JUST IN CASE I DIE

Just in Case I Die

RACHEL NORBY

Rachel Norby

Contents

For Josh, Paisley, and Auggie,

who daily remind me that

life is precious and should never

be taken for granted

Fiction is the lie that helps us understand the truth.
-TIM O'BRIEN, AUTHOR

Then you will know the truth,
and the truth will set you free.
-John 8:32 NIV

Before: The Author's Challenge

Before you finish reading this book, I could be dead. You could be dead. Someone you love could be dead, and by then, it might be too late.

Too late for what? you may be wondering. Well, dear reader, too late to say the things you've always wanted to say but haven't.

How do I know this? I am human. You are human. Because this thread of humanity binds us all together, I know that we all leave certain things unsaid.

The "certain things" I speak of are the things within the recesses of the human heart that we feel intensely and want our loved ones to know. Things that we oftentimes have on the tips of our tongue, but then the moment passes and we stuff the words back down to their depths and lock them away with the key of silence.

Things like "I really, *really* love you, despite all that has happened" or "I forgive you, even though you have hurt me" or "I am so proud of the person you are becoming."

The problem is that these unsaid things have the power to sever chords of friendship, kinship, and intimacy between people. These unsaid things have the power to throw each of us into that vast and soul-battering sea called regret.

There *is* a power found in words. They have the power to heal, uplift, and unify. But, my friend, there is a flip side. There is also power in the *absence* of words. The absence of words has the power to make people feel unloved, to shatter people's faith in God and themselves, and to leave people questioning their identity and the goodness of humanity itself. Omission of words can take the light out of a life and leave in its departure a pervasive darkness.

Why don't we *say* the things to our loved ones that we feel so intensely within? Moreover, why don't we *write down* the things we want them to remember when we are gone? That, dear reader, is the just-in-case-I-die challenge that I leave with you today—a challenge that became real for many people with the threat of the worldwide pandemic and became personal for me when I heard the words "possible cancer" uttered at a recent doctor's appointment. As you read the following chapters—each telling the story of a person who finds the courage to say the *certain things* that are deep within—I hope you wrestle with that challenge and find the courage to *say* the things that you have been wanting to say to the people who have been desperately waiting to hear them.

Before it's too late.

Chapter 1

Nick

I am finally back to being me. Nick. (Fully capable) adult. (Brilliant) engineer. (Once upon a time) loving husband. (Would have been) protective and supportive father. Finally back from the depths of hell, a.k.a. the years that the demon alcohol stole from me.

Now my only family is my Alcoholics Anonymous group. I see my "family" once a week, which used to feel like too much back when I didn't think I had a problem and begrudgingly attended, but now feels like not enough since everyone and everything that I cared about has been pushed away. The problem is that this family isn't really mine. I can't come home to them each day. I can't look them in the eyes daily and tell them that I love them. I can't hold them in my arms and feel the warmth of their love spreading to my heart. I lost that privilege a long time ago, and I fear I can never get it back. I fear I don't have the right to even *hope* to get that back. I simply don't deserve it after what I have done to them.

What a deceiver you are, Alcohol. What a normalized, unobtrusive liar cloaked in sleek-looking bottles and mesmerizingly shiny cans. How carefree and laid-back the commercials make you look, positioned in every societally-deemed attractive young person's hand, making every party a real party and not causing any major problems because of the "drink responsibly" tagline said in a rushed voice at the end. How readily available you are at grocery and convenience stores, liquor stores and bars in every town, and in coolers with the token red Solo cups at virtually every get-together. How smooth you taste on the way down and how acidic and wretched you are coming back up after a night of "too much" fun. How easily you worm your way into people's lives, making your tunnels underneath the facade of even ground for so long until the earth starts crumbling inward. That's when I really noticed it. Things and people started crumbling and slipping away from me. My thoughts. Birthdays and anniversaries. Social engagements. My job. My house. My wife. My future child. My faith. My future. Me. In that order. Alcohol stole it all, little by little, until there was nothing left to slip away.

The ironic thing is that I used to despise the taste of alcohol. I specifically remember being a seventeen-year-old teenager at a party that my parents were holding. As usual, the adults were drinking and underagers were either running around like squirrels (if under thirteen) or reclining in a chair watching the increasingly inebriated adults try to play yard games (if over thirteen). That was when my uncle, John, whom we had all dubbed "the cool uncle," leaned over and handed me a beer when my parents weren't looking, whispering, "If you want to be a real man, you need to learn to like this stuff."

With a conspiratorial wink and succinct head nod, he went back to playing bean bags with my parents. I promptly put the beer in my hoodie pocket and discreetly told my other cousins that we should "go look at something behind the shed." We proceeded to split the can, and when I was told to finish it, I tried to look cool like a "real man" and down it, but it tasted so horrible that inwardly I recoiled in disgust.

So much for being a real man. After that, I avoided alcohol like I used to avoid my annoying little sister when I was younger.

Then I hit college. Pete and Tony, my two roommates in my college dorm at Michigan State University, convinced me that alcohol was an acquired taste and that I needed to try it again. Peer pressure, combined with my need to prove myself, drove me to drink more and more throughout the year. Sure enough, I did acquire a taste for it. It started with a few weekends a month and turned into nearly every weekend. Not only did the frequency increase, but the volume.

Ironically, I met Hope at one of those parties toward the end of my freshman year, back when I had my drinking "under control." My buddy Pete was hosting a party at his nearby house because his parents were gone on vacation. It was an early spring, something every Midwesterner hopes for and rarely gets to witness. Like Lord Capulet in *Romeo and Juliet*, Pete was throwing a party to celebrate the arrival of spring, or "springtime beauty season" as he called it because the girls shed their enormous sweaters in favor of tank tops and shorts, and he had a massive pool in his backyard ready to celebrate this transformation.

I remember talking with Pete and Tony by the poolside when Hope walked up with Leah, a friend from our dorm. I had never seen Hope before, and as she turned to face us, it was her eyes that captivated me. They were a bright blue, matching the intensity of the summer sky, but with the softness of the sunset around the edges, drawing me in and momentarily hypnotizing me. By the time I realized I was staring, I heard Pete's voice saying, "Nick? Anyone home? This is Leah's cousin, Hope." I blinked, temporarily released from the spell her eyes had cast on me.

As I turned back to her, she offered a smile and a shy wave of her hand, and I found that I couldn't focus on anything else but her. I offered to show her around, and as we walked around the grounds getting to know each other, the spark I had felt when first meeting her started burning into a full-fledged flame. From that moment on, we were inseparable. Her blue eyes were my last thought at night and my first thought every morning. Asking her to marry me was one of the easiest and surest decisions I had ever made in my life.

We married the summer after we graduated college, celebrating with friends and family on the shore of Lake Michigan, the sunshine sparkling in Hope's eyes mirroring the glittering water around us, our hopes and dreams bolstered in our wedded bliss. We moved into a small starter home near the lake, and our first few years were spent renovating our house into a home while enjoying the simplicity of simply being loved by someone else.

Then my drinking started to take over my life, little by little. I not only drank on the weekends with our friends like I did in college, but I started drinking occasionally during the week. It started with a beer or two while in the recliner watching the game. Then it became an additional beer or two before bed. Eventually, I couldn't go a day without drinking. I started putting alcohol in my beverages at work. That's when I knew there was a problem, but I couldn't stop it at that point, despite the pleading from Hope.

My boss, Nate, eventually noticed and talked to me multiple times about getting help, which I refused because I thought I could control it. He finally was forced to let me go because my performance was compromised. This led to us getting behind on our house payments, causing even more arguments between us at home.

Then, one night, shortly after losing my job and while in the process of losing our house, in the midst of a heated argument after a night of drinking, I slapped her.

I hit my wife. My love. My Hope. The woman I had promised to love and to cherish. The look of shock on her face was mirrored only by my own. I remember looking at my hand, as if my hand had a brain and had made the decision on its own to hit her. She flashed me a look that told me it was over and moved out the next week. Just like that. She was gone. The divorce papers came shortly after. That was far worse than losing my job and the house. Jobs and homes can be replaced. People cannot.

Now, ten years later, I am finally sober. The demon alcohol robbed me out of more than a decade of my life. It ravaged my faith in other people and myself. It stole the people I loved the most. Now, I am working on forgiving myself, but I desperately want the forgiveness of my wife, as well. The only problem is that I have no idea where she is right now. She could be in Australia for all I know. My only hope at this point is divine intervention.

I don't openly share this with many people, but I have recently become a sucker for romantic comedies. My favorite one is *Message in a Bottle*, which I have watched (by myself now) multiple times in the past few years. I love the idea that a person can write all of his (or her) thoughts down, and it could be received by someone–maybe even the intended reader–somewhere in the world. With that miniscule but ever-present chance in my mind, I've written my own message in a bottle for my lost love:

My Blue-Eyed Hope,

How I have missed you. There isn't a day that goes by where I don't look for you. It's like a perpetual game of hide and seek, except I am always the seeker and never the finder.

It starts when I wake up. I look over at your side of the bed, wanting you to be there but realizing that I don't dare hope that you are. Something I took for granted all of those years has now become something akin to my deepest desire.

Once I realize that you're not there, I resignedly get up, scanning the hall and the bathroom for any sign of you. There are still two toothbrushes in the holder. Did you know that you left your toothbrush here? You must have been in a hurry to leave because I remember you commenting how you had finally found the "perfect" toothbrush. Too bad you didn't have the perfect husband to go with it. The day you left, I remember holding your toothbrush and sobbing. I tried to convince myself that you didn't truly leave because you wouldn't have left your toothbrush behind. What I really meant was that you wouldn't leave our love behind, but it was easier to focus on something tangible.

After checking the bathroom, I walk down the steps, my hand on the banister, peeking around the corner at the breakfast nook with the sun streaming in the window, hoping you will be there cradling your coffee mug in your hand, still in your pajamas, enjoying that time of still, sweet solace of morning. How you so loved the early morning, even more so after I became a raging alcoholic and the sweet hours of dawn became your time to recuperate your soul after a night of verbal litany from me. Every time I see the breakfast nook, I try to make you materialize before my eyes and imagine the conversations we might have had if I hadn't driven you to leave. Unfortunately, my imagination isn't strong enough to bring the real you back to me, which is all I ever want these days.

Everywhere I go, I look for signs of you. The problem is that the signs are everywhere, and that has made me realize something important. Some people fill life up, adding vibrancy and color to everything. That's you. The color maker. The beauty creator. You added so much vitality to our marriage and our lives. I think that's why I missed you so much after you left. I felt like a punctured balloon with all of the air seeping out. I was left trying to put my finger over the opening, but it was useless. The damage had already been done. You were gone. And so I keep on searching for you, but it seems I am destined to forever be the seeker of my blue-eyed beauty.

I know I've told you about how Uncle John handed me a beer when I was a teenager and told me that I needed to learn to like alcohol in order to be a "real man." It has taken me years to realize how wrong he was. Here is what I've discovered about being a real man. Real men don't listen to lies from other people, even if the liar is someone you care about and is seemingly well-intentioned. Real men don't let a substance take over their lives, even if the substance itself is socially acceptable. (I don't even touch alcohol any more–I view it as poison.) Real men guard their relationships and protect them, especially those they have promised to love. Real men can admit when they've made a mistake and apologize while taking strides to repair the damage that was done.

This is my apology letter. I am so sorry, more sorry than you will ever know. The kind of sorry that makes my gut ache deep within. I look at what I did to you and almost can't believe that was me, but I know that it was. All I know is that I love you more than I could ever fully express in words and I hope that you are happy. If, by chance, God directs this letter to you, know that you are still loved deeply by your adoring (ex) husband. I remain grateful for the brief time that we had together and for the joy that you brought to my life. Missing your blue eyes every day.

Forever Yours,

Nick

Chapter 2

Jade

I don't even know where to begin because I don't know how this started and how this is going to end. I am just...confused. Confused, but still me. Jade, the green-eyed girl, the one my momma called precious like the stone for which I was named. She also told me that jade is a stone that promotes wisdom, balance, and peace, but if that is true, then she should have named me some-thing else. I have not been wise. My life is not balanced. I feel anything but peace lately.

Do you remember being a kid and making a snow-man? You start with this little snowball, and once you keep rolling it, the ball keeps getting bigger and bigger until you need to put the ball on top of the other one but discover you can't because it's too heavy. I feel like that's what happened to me. The snowball got too big and too heavy for me, and now I am sitting here in the snow, defeated, looking at the snowball and trying to decide what to do. Do I keep trying? Ask for help? Just go back inside?

No one grows up thinking, *I am going to cheat on my spouse when I grow up.* I have despised cheaters my entire life. In high school, there was this girl who was ranked in the top three of our class who cheated in nearly every class. I despised her. I had to work hard to earn my grades, and she skated by everyone else by copying her classmates' homework. As a teenager, I felt repulsed towards anyone who cheated on a boyfriend or girlfriend. The cheater's name would never be considered in the running for the next candidate in my future boyfriend campaign. "Once a cheater, always a cheater" is a saying I believed for the longest time. Now I am not so sure.

I've had an enviable life. My husband, Jack, has always loved me with an unceasing love and has always made life...easy. Perhaps too easy. My three girls are the joy of my life, each with a distinct personality that gives the entrée of life a unique flavor. My job has always been one that has fulfilled me and challenged me. Now everything is on the precipice of a very large cliff, and I don't know how to balance it all without crashing to the depths of the canyon below.

Why, oh why, did I accept that friend request online? It seemed innocent enough at the time. A former boyfriend from more than twenty years ago? I even ran it by Jack, and he laughed about it and told me he didn't care if I friended Mitch. Jack's not laughing now. Neither am I. Come to think of it, neither is Mitch.

Now it has snowballed into something I don't recognize and something I don't know how to control. I now know things about both men that I can't unknow. I love both men for completely different reasons, and my heart is being ripped in two entirely opposite directions. I have one foot in each camp but can't sustain life much longer that way. When I'm with Jack, I feel swayed to stay with him and try to pick up the pieces of my old life. When I'm with Mitch, I am consumed by the ferocity of his love and can't escape it.

If I am being honest, though I care greatly for him, part of me is angry with Mitch for contacting me again and being willing to break up my marriage. But the blame doesn't rest solely on him. I allowed this to happen, and I have to take responsibility for it. If I could rewind time and go back to that point of contact, I would. The thing about time is that we can't rewind. We can only go forward. And not fast-forward. We don't have the option of passing over the painful parts that our decisions have caused. Oh, how I wish I could skip ahead to see how this story ends because I am tired of hurting every single day. I am tired of seeing the utter destruction that my decisions have caused. I am weary of seeing the glassy, faraway look in Jack's eyes because the pain has sucked out the marrow of his happiness. I can't bear to see the repercussions of my decisions in my three girls' lives. The girls have had so many questions and tears. Fits of anger. Lashing out. Trouble focusing at school. If I can't even understand why I have done this horrible thing, how can I expect them to understand? The answer is: I can't.

It took a little while for people in town to catch on to what was going on, but I know now that they know. I know everyone is talking about me, and I know what they are saying because I have thought the same things about myself. "What was she thinking?" *I wasn't.* "I would have never expected this to happen to *them.*" *Me neither.* "Jack deserves better. If I were him, I'd kick her right out." *If I were him, I would, too.* I can't disagree with any of them. I can take their gossip, but I don't want it to affect Jack and the girls. I have already caused them enough pain without the judgment and pity of the entire town.

The problem is that I'm stuck. I am sitting by the snowballs of my decisions and can't seem to decide what to do. I pray every day, pleading with God to help me out of the mess that I've created. I have become the monster I most despised for the majority of my life, and I don't know how to un-become. I am the thing that I hate.

The irony of it all is that I really do love Jack and the girls. I didn't do this because of a lack of love. No matter what happens, I need them to know how sorry I am and how I truly feel about them. I can't always say the things aloud that I feel the most, so I wrote down a few things that were on my heart to say:

My Loves,

I know that you will be reading this with mixed feelings. I know you love me, but I know part of you hates what I have done. I hate what I have done, too, and all I can say is that I love you and that I am sorry.

***Jack**—If I could go back in time, I would say "no" to Mitch's friend request. I had no idea what problems it would cause. I allowed this to happen, and I have to take responsibility for it. I can't reverse time and I can't undo my mistake, but I can say that I am sorry. More sorry than you can ever understand. All you have done is to love me with an unceasing, utterly adoring love that made my life and our life together easy. I have tested that love beyond the acceptable bounds of marriage, and I hope that, in time, you can forgive me for it. My heart hurts for what I have done to you and what I have done to us.*

No matter what happens, know that I love you. That might sound strange or untrue based on my decisions, but nonetheless, it is true and always will be true. You captured my heart in college and I couldn't wait to begin my life with you. Your love has always been so true, so steady, and I couldn't wait to build a life upon that solid foundation. What a beautiful life we have built together. Even though I have broken things (including your heart and mine), we can still be proud of the love that we have had and the three beautiful girls that have come out of it. I will never regret one moment I have spent with you. I have always and will always love you.

Emma, Katelyn, and Jilly*—No matter what has happened, know that I still love you with the fierceness of a tiger. None of what has happened is your fault or your father's fault. I simply made a mistake and have made a mess of things. I hope that, in time, you can forgive me.*

You three girls have been the light and the joy of my life. Even through the chaotic days when you three were all under five years old, the days of diapers, tantrums, and spilled milk at every meal, you three always said or did something every day that would make me smile. Not just smile, but laugh with my whole body. You know, the belly-shaking, side-grabbing, gasping-for-breath sort of laugh. As you grew older, I was amazed at what you learned in such a short span of time and how you changed, sometimes even within the course of one day. You metamorphosed before my very eyes and have become three very distinctly beautiful butterflies. My mariposas.

I have one thing that I desperately want to tell you. I know you probably feel that I am not the right one to dispense wisdom right now, but this is something important. Don't be afraid to love because of what has happened. Your father and I have loved each other deeply, and I will never regret that. I have three beautiful girls and many wonderful memories that I will forever cherish from it. Don't be afraid to love someone fully and let them love you in return. Love is still out there and is all around us. Don't let my one mistake drive you away from love.

You are my precious girls, and nothing will ever change that. Know that no matter what has happened or what will happen, my love for you can never be severed, not even by my mistakes.

Forever Love,

Jade

Chapter 3

[Coach] Nova

Who am I now that I'm not who I used to be? That is the question. I've gotten so wrapped up in what I have done the last twenty years that I have forgotten who I am without the title "COACH" attached to me. The accident has forced me to think about such things.

After I graduated from college and started teaching and coaching, I've been Coach Novus, Nova for short, to everyone around me. I've always loved my last name. My parents told me, ever since I was young, that "novus" means "new" in Latin. They always reminded me that I was something fresh and new to the world around me. Mom and Dad gave me the nickname Nova while I was growing up, which I liked even better than my last name. A "nova" is a star that has suddenly become intensely bright, which fits my personality perfectly. I have always had what some people might call "an excess of energy," which wore out my parents and energized my friends growing up. In fact, when I was playing sports, which my parents put me into so I could burn off some of my extra "pizzazz" (as my Uncle Rob called it), I could always play through an entire game without tiring. Sometimes, during the latter part of a game when the rest of my teammates would be shutting down mentally and physically, I would get all fired up and shout encouraging comments out like bullets, which earned me the nickname "Supernova" throughout my school career.

I can honestly say that I have loved my life—all 43 years of it. How many people can say that in this world? Not many. So many people seek "happiness" like it's a treasure hunt with an elusive jewel that cannot be attained, but what they don't realize is that the treasure is right there in front of them: the life they have and the people they love in it. That was something my parents always emphasized while I was growing up and it stuck, and now I try to impress that same ideal onto my children. They, along with my wife, are my treasure on this side of heaven, and I try to treat them accordingly (though I am human and slip up once in a while, as my wife is sure to point out). They have supported me throughout my teaching and coaching career, and continue to support me in this post-accident world that I am currently navigating.

Social studies teaching. Football. Basketball. Baseball. My working life from August through early June. Like clockwork, the beginning of football season eased me back into the coaching world before school began each year. Basketball helped the long Midwest winters to pass by more quickly in a flurry of weeknight games and weekend tournaments. Baseball signified the start of spring and brought the smells of freshly cut grass, hot dogs, and popcorn that carried me right into the summer weeks that I had off to spend with my family. Yes, it has been a wonderful life, but now I find myself at a loss of how to face a life that has been completely altered.

The accident. It all comes back to that day. Just like many of the days of my life, I was driving to the high school to coach my basketball boys, the mighty Mustangs, in a weekend tournament during Christmas break. They were ready, as was I. I prepped them mentally and physically for the caliber of opponents we would be facing. We practiced the fundamentals until they were gasping for breath, implemented a few new plays that would confuse the competition, and analyzed film to learn the strengths and weaknesses of our main opponents. I was pumped and ready to coach, eating my typical pre-game breakfast of eggs and toast smothered with homemade jam and blaring my pump-me-up music in the car on the way to the high school. Perhaps my mind was off the road. Maybe I wasn't paying close enough attention. Maybe my music was too loud and I couldn't hear it. All I remember is driving forward after looking both ways at the stop sign right before everything went black.

How did I not see the truck that hit me? Even if the dark gray color of it did match the road, I still should have noticed a *moving vehicle*. It hit me going over 60 miles an hour, flattening the front of my car before flipping it multiple times. I've been told by the rescue workers on the scene that it was a miracle I survived. Apparently, the vehicle was the worst they had seen in years. In fact, as one of them told me while I was in the hospital later, they took one look at the vehicle and assumed whoever was in the vehicle was dead, but protocol mandated that they check for survivors anyway. After the initial surprise of finding me (barely) alive, they utilized the Jaws of Life just to get me out. They were extremely careful as they put my broken body on the stretcher, but the damage had already been done. My spinal cord was severed in a way that would leave me forever a paraplegic.

When I woke up in the local hospital two days later, the tear-stained faces of my wife and kids told me the news before I noticed that my legs didn't work. My wife, Joy—who was very appropriately named by her parents, I might add—had an uncharacteristically morose expression on her face as she squeezed my hand upon my waking. When I found my voice, I said, "Is it really that bad?" She nodded sadly and whispered the news into my ear. My heart sank into the depths of my badly bruised chest. Like a filmstrip that I was forced to watch, I was instantly inundated with flashing images of things that I would never do again. Run around with my kids. Go for a run with my dog. Join a game of pick-up basketball. Garden with my wife. Waterski. Play summer baseball. Coach. How would one go about coaching from the constraints of a wheelchair? For some reason, this final image stuck in my brain as I tried to hold back the tears in front of my family. My life, as I knew it, would be completely different from this point on.

I've often heard the saying that one instant can change a person's life. Though I always believed it, I always applied it to the positive things that change the trajectory of a person's life. Meeting someone and falling in love. The birth of a child. A medical miracle. An influential teacher. An inspirational coach. I guess I never thought much about the negative outcomes of that statement, and I most definitely did not think that anything of that magnitude would ever happen to *me*. That kind of stuff only happened to *other* people. Ironically, now I was the "other people" to other people.

As I lay there reflecting while my wife stroked my hand, all of the versions of my last name came to my mind. Novus: "new." Nova: "a star that suddenly increases in brightness and then fades to its former obscurity over time." (The latter part of that definition I had pretty much ignored all of my life, but I couldn't right now.) Supernova: "a star that suddenly increases its brightness because of a catastrophic explosion that ejects most of its mass." Like a nova, had I burned brightly and now I would fade into obscurity? Were all of my bright years behind me? Like a supernova, had I ejected most of my mass from the catastrophic explosion that happened when our two vehicles collided?

The mental battle for purpose and control raged on within my mind, but then I made a decision: I had always been an optimistic person, so I would *choose* to be a combination of all the positive aspects of my name. Much of life is determined by our choices, is it not? Isn't that one of the ideals I had pounded into my children and students day after day? Yes, I would choose to see a new version of myself. **Novus: "new."** My different life, from the seat of a wheelchair, would be a new world for me to explore and enjoy. **Nova: "a star that suddenly increases in brightness and then fades to its former obscurity over time."** NOW was my time to increase in brightness. I would fade into "former obscurity" only at death. **Supernova: "a star that suddenly increases its brightness because of a catastrophic explosion that ejects most of its mass."** I had ejected "the mass" of the use of my legs, but because of it, I would now burn brilliantly, a dazzling spectacle of brightness for the remaining years of my life.

Yes, I decided then and there that I would take the poet Walt Whitman's stance that he made in the 19th century: "hoping to cease not till death." My supernova days were just beginning. After the doctor and medical staff came in to explain more specifics about the accident, I turned to my wife and asked for a pen and paper. She gave me a questioning look, her eyebrows raised quizzically, and I said, "I want to write a letter. To my students and athletes. For the school newspaper." She smiled and located them for me, and I began to write:

To my Students and Athletes:

I should be dead right now. From the mouths of the rescue workers, they didn't expect to find anyone alive in the obliterated vehicle of mine that they found on the side of the road that day. But I am alive. God spared me, and I firmly believe it's for a reason.

Things will be different now. I will continue to teach, but from the seat of a wheelchair. I won't be able to jump on top of tables and desks like I used to, but I will be able to wheel around like a madman to deliver the content of my lessons. Expect that. I still have a lot of energy to burn off and a passion for history, so I'm not letting something like a wheelchair get in the way. As I always tell you all in class, "Make it happen."

As for coaching, I am unsure at this point of what I will be able to do. I plan to finish out the basketball season, as I know that I will be able to wheel around on the basketball court floor during practice and coach from the side of the court, like usual, during the games, but I have yet to figure out how life in a wheelchair will translate into coaching football or baseball. I have to speak to my family and to school administration to figure things out. Until then, press on. Whether I am able to coach you or not, I will always believe in you boys and fully support you. You are the leaders of tomorrow and will continue to do great things. Believe that and make it happen.

There is one thing I ask of you: Treat me like you've always treated me. I am not feeling sorry for myself and don't need your pity. I need your support. I still have full use of my (sometimes quirky) brain and most of my body, and I won't let you forget it. I am choosing to live life to the fullest and to cease not until death. I hope you choose to do the same with whatever challenges you may be facing.

Making it happen,

Mr. Novus a.k.a. Nova

After I finished writing, I handed the letter to my wife. As she read it, a few tears trickled down her cheeks, and she promised that she would submit it in time for the next edition of the school newspaper.

As it was Christmas break, I was able to recuperate in the hospital for about a week and rest for a week at home (per doctor's orders, even though I wanted to go back to school right away) without taking too many days off from school.

When I arrived at school for the first time since my accident, I couldn't help but be overwhelmed—in a good way—about the support that I felt from my staff and students. After driving my newly renovated, handicap-accessible vehicle to the staff parking lot, I found that the administration had put a sign that said "Mr. Nova's VIP

Parking" on the chain-linked fence in front of the parking space closest to our building. No handicap symbol, just a sign. That alone brought a smile to my face, but that was only the start. As I wheeled into the doorway after pushing the handicap button (thanks to our referendum that had finally passed, all of our new building's doors were handicap accessible), I saw little posters made by students lining the walls, saying things like "Welcome back, Nova!" and "We missed you, Coach!" on them. I couldn't have wiped the enormous smile off my face if I tried. Thankfully, my classroom was on the first floor right across from the office, which saved my arms from extra wheeling, and as I turned the corner, the office staff was lined up (they must have been watching the cameras for me) to give me high fives and hugs.

I thought I was holding it together pretty well until I went into my classroom with Mr. Nelson, the high school principal. As we entered my classroom, I looked around to see even more of the encouraging signs that had begun in the hallway and trailed all the way into my room. Somewhat in awe of the support that I was feeling, I wheeled into my desk area and couldn't believe what I saw. There, on my desk, was an enormous pile of envelopes.

I attempted to ask Mr. Nelson about them, but before I could get the words out, he said, "They are letters from staff, students, and athletes. We published the letter that you wrote in the hospital in the school newspaper and sent it out via email to everyone at the high school, and these are the responses. As you can see, there are quite a few of them."

I smiled back at him with tears in my eyes. "I think I received more letters than Santa did this year."

Mr. Nelson patted me on the shoulder. "Well, you would at least give him a run for his money." He paused for a moment before turning to leave. "We are all truly happy to have you back, Nova. School just wasn't the same without you. Let me know if you need anything."

After he left to attend to the daily chaos that was sure to ensue in the high school office, I turned my attention to the pile of letters on my desk. I found a bag to house them all in order to clear my desk for my upcoming classes, but I couldn't resist pulling out just one to read before school started. The outside of the envelope simply had "Coach" written on it. As I opened the envelope, I pulled out a handwritten letter, which was a miracle in itself in this age of technology. As I started to read the following words, I couldn't keep the tears from falling:

Dear Coach,

Sam here. I am not sure if I have ever written a real letter before, but if anyone was worthy of me busting out my handwriting skills, it's you, Coach. So here goes.

I want you to know that you are an inspiration to me and our entire school, and it's not just because you survived the accident. (Sorry for the language, but that was pretty badass of you. All of the basketball guys were like, "Yeah, it takes more than a car accident to take Coach Nova down!") You inspire all of us with your life. You always see the bright side of things and help all of us to do the same. Like the time that my ex-girlfriend broke up with me and I was moping around at practice. You called me over and told me how much money I would be saving by being single and how I would have way more time to hang out with the guys. Then you reminded me of how she had attempted to make chocolate chip cookies for the team and how they were rock hard, and you said, "If that's not a sign that it wasn't meant to be, I don't know what is." You got me laughing so hard that I couldn't help but enjoy the rest of practice.

I am guessing that many people who face something as life-altering as your car accident get down on themselves and on life, focusing on all of the things they will never be able to do again, but not you. You came out of it thinking of all of the things you could and would do. That inspires all of us. If you can keep going and not give up after what happened to you, then the rest of us feel like we can tackle our problems head-on and still make a great life. Like you are always saying, "Make it happen." You are making it happen, Coach, and I think it's awesome.

I just saw this movie recently that had a bird called a Phoenix rising from the ashes after its "death." That's how I picture you, Coach. You are rising from the ashes after your accident like some kind of amazing miracle. You're the kind of guy who will go on to do things like paraplegic marathons or something. I can totally picture it. Thanks for inspiring us all, Coach!

- Sam

P.S. My Grandma Rose is praying for you, and that's pretty serious business. No one messes with Grandma Rose. She's like a prayer warrior or something.

I set the letter down after wiping a few tears from my cheeks. Good old Sam. I knew I always liked that kid.

I considered the words that he said. A Phoenix. Rising from the ashes. Me. I couldn't help but smile as the first bell rang.

Chapter 4

Rue

I was too young to fully know what I was doing, but now I can't forget what I have done. There are too many reminders out there. Most daytime television ads have small children in them, whether the little ones need wet wipes to clean them up or kitchen wipes to clean up the messes that were left behind. When I drive, I see "Save the Babies" billboards left and right along the freeways. When I have a doctor or dentist appointment, the waiting area is often full of young children playing with toys or reading books. Little reminders are everywhere, and each one tugs on my heart just a little bit more until one day my heart will be yanked out by all the tugging and I am afraid I will die from it all.

Death is the one great equalizer that no human can escape. The carriage of death–as Emily Dickinson put it in one of her poems–comes for each one of us. Some of us are ready for it and many of us are not. For some it comes too soon and for others, too late. Some people have a say in when it happens to them and others have that decision made for them...like I made for the little one who could have been in my life. Unfortunately, our mortality is something we all must face.

I have always liked country music. The power of story is so evident in most country songs, especially the ballads. There is an old country song with the line, "I wish I didn't know now what I didn't know then," but I would change the lyrics to, "I wish I knew back then what I do know now." Wisdom really is wasted on the old. If I could go back to my younger self, I would tell her many things. I would tell her that she is beautiful just the way she is. I would tell her that she doesn't need a man to make her feel complete. I would tell her to go for her goals in life and not get sidetracked by other things and other people who will entangle her. I would explain what true sexual freedom is and what it is not: It's NOT having sex wherever and whenever someone else wants you to, but it IS having the freedom to say "no" to all of the raging hormonal nitwits when the time isn't right and to wait for a committed relationship where both people are invested in each other and the future. Then you aren't left with empty "I love you's" that are really "I want you's" and you aren't left alone and pregnant. You aren't left scared out of your mind with nowhere to turn. That is what I didn't know then that I do know now. But now it's too late.

What's ironic is that now I would love to have a child. Fortunately for me, I met Robert–my sweet, dashing man who loves me with all of my baggage–through a co-worker who had a feeling we would be compatible. We married when I was twenty-nine (just before my self-proposed goal of being married by thirty), but we've had...complications. After trying for a child for five years with no results, we started consulting a doctor who ran some tests. It turns out that Robert is sterile.

Though I tried my best to sway him, Robert didn't feel comfortable with adoption, so we have been left childless. Sometimes I feel like it is a just punishment for the child's life that I took when I was a teenager, but in my heart of hearts, I don't think God really operates that way. At least I hope not.

Robert is the only person I have ever told about my abortion. I am just too ashamed to tell anyone else. In hindsight, after years of mulling it over in my brain, I have concluded that the real debate about abortion is actually over whether or not it's *permissible*, which is completely different than the typical discussion of whether it's morally right or wrong. Being both permissible by law and expedient, when someone feels scared out of her mind at the prospect of the future with no help in raising a child, that is all she thinks about and has to deal with the moral complications later. The ethical dilemma is something she is left to think about for the rest of her life. In my experience, it is an inner wound that takes years to heal.

Regret comes in many forms. The ache in my heart whenever I see a sweet young cherub playing on the playground. The shallowness of breath whenever I see a child the same age as mine would have been if she had lived. The emptiness in my arms when I see a mother rocking her child and I have nothing in mine. The tears that fall involuntarily and unknowingly when I'm at the cinema and a child enters a particular scene. The hope that is shattered when I realize I will never have a child, and thus will never have a grandchild in the future.

I know this might sound strange, but to deal with my grief over my baby's death, I have started and kept a diary written and devoted entirely to her. Yes, the baby was a girl. I just know it. I don't know how I know, but I know. Call it mother's intuition. I named her Rose and I write to her periodically, especially when I am feeling remorseful.

I have kept this journal for years. I am not sure what I will do with it in the end, since the intended reader is obviously elsewhere, but writing it has been a form of catharsis for my aching heart. I simply *needed* to tell Rose all that was pent up within me so I could begin to heal.

Here are a few of my earlier entries:

May 6th

My Sweet Rose,

I am so sorry. If saying "I'm sorry" could undo what I have done, I would say it a million times over. In fact, when I was in the clinic getting the procedure done, I wanted to stop halfway through and undo everything. But it was too late. Words cannot capture my remorse.

*Rose, do you know what "Rue" means? It means to **bitterly regret** something. How perfectly my mother named me. I don't just regret what I have done to you...I bitterly regret it. I am angry at myself, angry at HIM (he who shall not be named who left me alone and pregnant), angry at the world. I am hoping the bitterness will dissipate with time, but now it consumes every part of me: my thoughts, my words, my actions, my sense of goodness in the world, my hope in the future. How could I allow an innocent babe to die because of a choice that I made? Sometimes I try to convince myself that you sacrificed yourself for me so my future could be better, but I am never able to fully believe my own argument. For it to be a true sacrifice, the sacrifice has to be willing. You weren't willing. You weren't even aware of what was going on. I robbed you of your ability to choose life. I robbed myself of the opportunity to see someone treasure you. I am the worst kind of thief.*

How do I even sign this?

Me

May 12th

My Daughter Rose,

It's Mother's Day today. When I was young, Mother's Day seemed like such a happy day to me. My mother was beaming as my siblings and I gave her gifts (usually home-made) and showered her with "I love you" kisses. My dad convinced us to do little chores around the house to make things easier for Mom on her special day, and we did them without complaint, like it was some secret mission that we were all accomplishing together. Mission "Make Mom Feel Loved" was in full force every Mother's Day at our house.

Now, Mother's Day just feels...empty. Not just empty. More like a meteorite came down and left a crater where everything used to be, burning holes through the layers of goodness and human decency and hope, leaving every-thing burning in its wake. Is this how the dinosaurs felt be-fore extinction? Is my soul going extinct?

Rue

P.S. I tried writing "Mommy," but couldn't bring myself to do it...

July 1st

My Darling Rose,

I haven't written for a few months. I have been in a dark place. It's like living in the cold northern tundra where you don't see the sun for a season...only darkness. This is my season of darkness, but I am hoping for some sunlight soon.

I keep thinking that the pain of losing you is way worse than the trouble it would have been to give birth to you. I could have put you up for adoption and gifted you to a loving couple. Maybe they would have let me visit you with some sort of open adoption agreement. Or maybe...I could have kept you and raised you. There is no way that all of the dirty diapers, lack of sleep, and general daily stress would be worse than living in the self-imposed vacuum where I now reside. I have graduated now with all of my "unlimited opportunities" (as my high school counselor put it), but I don't feel the pull of any of those opportunities enough to act on them. I am "frittering away" (as my mom calls it) at the local community college, hoping something will "speak to me" soon. The only voices I hear are my own telling me things I would rather not write down.

I have asked God to forgive me, but now I need to work on forgiving myself. Why is that always so much harder? Why are many of us so willing to extend forgiveness to others that we won't extend to ourselves? Sigh. I will keep working on it.

Rue

October 5th

Eternally Loved Rose,

I love you. It's strange that I can love so strongly some-one who was only a part of me for a short while. Perhaps that is it. You were (and still are, apparently, since I can't get you out of my mind) a part of me. A part. Of me. Not apart from me. (Why did I think that they could just take you out of me and I would feel...nothing? How did I even think that things could just go back to normal? Things have felt anything but normal afterwards. Emptiness is the new normal, and I despise it.)

Yes, I started loving you when you were inside of me, and now I'm afraid that I just can't stop. I once read a book that said love can't be stopped by death. Now I truly believe it. Death never hindered my love for you. In fact, it may have amplified it, since people have a tendency to feel more strongly about the people who are lost to them. You are permanently lost but forever loved by me.

Love Forever,

Me

May 6

My Perfect Rosebud,

It's been one year since you died. One whole year. So much has changed since then. I can't explain it. My life is this odd paradox of perpetual inner numbness yet feeling everything too deeply. I stare off into the distance, viewing nothing but seeing everything. Tears fall without any provocation. The things I used to care so much about now hold no meaning for me, and the things I could care less about before now have become paramount.

I now see other people's pain as plain as day. The pain resides on their whole bodies. Yes, I said "on" instead of "in." Pain, to me, is outwardly visible. I see it in the way people walk, where the sadness of the soul has taken away the spring in their step. I see it in the vacant, glassy look in people's eyes as they stare at nothing in particular, too world-weary to shift their eyes. I see it in people's posture, where the lack of hope has put invisible weights on top of their shoulders and continually presses down, down, down, until people have sunk into their seats and have no desire to get up again. Once a person goes through a devastating loss, they become a cohabitant of the sphere in which pain resides. They are a fellow seer of communal misery.

My Rose. My beautiful Rose that would have bloomed in the garden of life. Cut from the garden. By me. When spring came around this year, I planted a rose bush, and it has little buds on it now. The color is a soft pink, which somehow reminds me of you. I can't wait for them to bloom. When the first one blooms, I think I shall sit and just stare at its beauty and take in its mesmerizing aroma. Its essence will remind me of you, and all I want to do is bask in its presence.

Perennially yours,

Rue

One of my most recent entries:

September 5

My (Would Be) Blooming Rose,

You would have been twenty this year. TWENTY. Can you believe it? I have been keeping this journal faithfully for the last twenty years. Some years I have written more frequently than others, but I have written more than 200 entries spanning these twenty lost years. It helps me feel close to you. I believe we all have souls, and though I was responsible for the death of your physical body, I have still felt and continually feel a connection with your soul. Keeping this journal connects my soul to yours.

Sometimes I play a game. I call it "Where Would Rose be Now?" (which makes me envision a bracelet imprinted with the letters WWRBN, much like the "What Would Jesus Do?" WWJD bracelets that were so popular at one point). Anyway, I played the game just this morning, and I envisioned you starting your second year of college some-where, majoring in something that would change the world in your own little way. I pictured you meeting some charming young man who would one day call and ask for permission to marry you. I saw myself walking you down the aisle toward said young man, looking handsome in his tuxedo, smiling lovingly at his radiant bride, both of you envisioning a life where you would grow old together. You should have had the chance at that dream. Sigh. I don't know if I should play that game any longer. It hurts my heart too much. It brings back the guilt that never quite goes away, kept at bay just below the surface of my sub-conscious.

Sometimes (always) I think about how different my life would have been had I kept you. The first few years would have been so hard, I admit, but then the reward would have come: I would physically have you with me now. You would come home to me when you had breaks or vacation time. We would shop together, picking out cute clothes and accessories for the both of us. We would cook together at holidays, filling the house with tantalizing aromas and filling our hearts with memories. We would have that bond that is unique to mothers and daughters. Is this how all mothers who have lost a daughter feel? Does the pain ever lessen? Are other mothers better at dealing with the pain than I am, or do we all just shove the pain down and grieve within, answering "I am well" with a fake smile when peo-ple ask how we are doing? Even the fake smile took a long time to locate. The real one was lost when I lost you.

Though it may not seem like it, I have forgiven myself. It took an interminable amount of time and a whole lot of divine intervention. I eagerly await the day where I will see you again. I hope aborted babies go to heaven, since that is where I envision being reunited with you. I have to warn you, though...I may never let go once I start hugging you. We may be permanently attached into eternity.

Looking forward to that day,

Your Loving Mother
(I feel like I can say that now! Look how far I have come!)

Chapter 5

Max[well]

Being in eighth grade stinks. Being in eighth grade without a father at home to talk about what is going on in stinkin' eighth grade stinks even more. To top it off, my English teacher (Blast those English teachers! They always want you to write something "meaningful"!) gave the class an assignment to write a letter to someone who has "impacted your life." She didn't say that the person needed to have *positively* impacted my life, so I chose to write to my "dad." Here goes...

Max[well] Anderson

Hour 5

September 28th

Impact Letter

Father,

I was going to start with the typical "Dear Dad," but I didn't want to start off with a lie. You aren't dear to me or to anyone in our family since you left us when I was just old enough to remember you. You also haven't been my dad. Other people have had to step into that role because you chose not to take it. If you've taught me anything, it is that anyone can be a father, but it takes someone dedicated to be called "Dad." That might sound bitter, but I'm just being honest.

You are probably wondering about why I wrote my name the way I did above in the heading. Did you know that I go by just "Max" now? Unfortunately, my teachers make me write my full name, but I write it Max[well] as my own small form of rebellion. I decided to drop the [well] for a few reasons. First, you always called me Maxwell. You always *insisted* that people call me my full name, though Mom and other people would have loved to call me "Max" or some other nickname. I would have welcomed a nickname. Nicknames imply...closeness and affection, neither of which I have felt from you since you left. Besides that, Max[well] implies that everything *is* well. Things are *not* well and they haven't been for a while. Mom works a lot of the time, so she isn't home as much as she would like to be. Sometimes I need help with my homework, and no one is home to help me. Even with working so much, she can barely pay the bills. There are a lot of things I would love to be able to do at school, but we don't have the extra money for me to do them. Did you know that there is a $100 participation fee for every junior high sport at school? Mom saves her extra money and lets me be in one sport each year, and I picked basketball because the school supplies the uniform and the ball. All I have to buy is a decent pair of shoes, which I am able to buy after saving money from doing yard work for the neighbors every summer. At least I have that. Playing basketball helps me forget about my problems. I'm actually pretty good at basketball (at least that's what Coach Peterson tells me). You'd know that if you came to a game sometime. I know it's kind of stupid since you've never actually shown up at anything in my entire life, but before every game, I scan the crowd to see if you are there. In one of our book discussions at school, my English teacher said that kids always want their parents to love and support them. I wish that weren't true because it stinks to want someone who doesn't want you back. Apparently, even crappy dads are better than no dads. Maybe someday you'll show up.

Do you remember that book we have at home called *Book of Questions*? Remember how we all used to flip through it and ask each other questions? Even as a five-year-old at the time, that memory has stuck in my brain as one of my few good memories from when we used to be a family. I remember how both you and Mom would laugh at the answers I gave, since apparently five-year-old answers are hilarious to adults. Anyway, we still have that book on the bookshelf in the living room. (Mom hasn't had the heart to get rid of it, since it must remind her of better times, too.) I flip through it every once in a while and ask Mom questions (if she's home) or just answer them myself if she's not. One of the recent ones was, "If you could ask your father or mother any one question, what would you ask?" I didn't have to think very long about that one because I know the questions that I would ask you: Why? Why did you leave us? I thought we were all so happy. Mom always tells me that it wasn't my fault that you left, but I still wonder. Was there something that I said or did to make you go? Was there something I could have done to make you stay? Mom says it's a lot more complicated than that, so it must be something that I can't figure out yet. For some reason, I feel like if I knew why you left, then maybe it wouldn't hurt so much. At least then I'd have a reason.

When I was younger and you called my name, it always sounded like "MaxWILL" with your Southern accent. In fact, I thought my name was Maxwill for a while. Now I find that ironic, since I think a more fitting name would have been Max[won't]. Your leaving has taught me a lot about what NOT to do in life and has made me decide that Max[WON'T] do the following things: I will not abandon my family. I will not work so much that I don't have time for my family. I will never say that I "don't have time" to do something with my kids when I have them in the future. I will not call my children by their full names. They get to have nicknames that they pick out themselves. I will not fail at school or at life because

I was dealt a rotten hand. Instead, I will succeed at whatever life throws at me because I want to prove that I can make it on my own—without your help, Dad, since you never offered it in the first place. I will not let what you have (or haven't) done keep me from having an awesome future. Those are the things that Max[won't] do.

Mom has told me that I need to forgive you. That's what my youth leader, Mike, says I need to do, too. I am trying. I am trying to forgive what you have done, but it is so hard. I have needed you and you haven't been there for me. I have wanted you in my life and you never even contacted me. That makes it hard to forgive. But I will try.

Maybe I'll see you again someday,

Max

*　　*　　*　　*　　*　　*　　*　　*　　*　　*　　*　　*

Mrs. Erickson,

I know you said the letter was only supposed to be one or two pages, but I hope you will make an exception for me. I have never really written down all my thoughts to my dad, and I guess I had a lot more to say than I thought. I hope you don't mind this one time. Also, please don't look at me any differently in class. I don't want or need your pity. Just treat me like you always have and we'll be good.

Max

P.S. After reading this, would you maybe let me start putting just "Max Anderson" on the top of my papers? Just wondering.

Chapter 6

Ruby

I know that I am slipping. I first noticed it when I kept losing things. I mean, I've always been a person who misplaced my keys, but when I started losing my phone, to-do lists, money, and generally anything that a person has to keep track of on a daily basis, I knew that something was wrong. My husband, Ronnie, once found the milk in the cupboard and the cereal in the refrigerator, and he turned to look at me with raised eyebrows. I knew then that he wondered about me, but he didn't say anything for the longest time. He was always so respectful of me like that, even when he had realized that I was slipping.

It was I who finally brought it up to him. One night, after lying restlessly in bed for what felt like hours, I cleared my throat and whispered, "Ronnie, are you still awake?"

He turned almost immediately, his back having been facing me, and whispered, "Yes. I can't sleep either."

I sighed deeply. I had been aching to talk to him about what was happening to me, but dreading it at the same time. Once I confessed my fears about what was happening to me, the problem really existed. Once I admitted that there was a problem, I couldn't un-speak the words. Once the words were out in the open, there was no turning back. That is the nature of words. Words have power and permanence. People forget this and throw them around carelessly, not realizing it is like slinging arrows that puncture and injure the innocent. Yes, I realized the gravity of what I was about to say, but it needed to be said.

I locked eyes with Ronnie, whose eyes I can find even in the darkest of rooms, and confessed, "I fear that there is something wrong with me."

Ronnie, always the jokester and continual room-brightener, said, "It only took you sixty years of marriage to finally admit that."

I laughed, breaking the tension of the moment, but my laughter slowly dissolved into tears. Tears that had been pent up for months. Tears that I had been withholding, trying to pretend that things were "just fine" and would get better. Tears of worry and anxiety about my future. They all started flooding out and I couldn't stop them. As my body convulsed with sobs, Ronnie pulled me close, knowing that I just needed to be held.

After my tears subsided, we talked for over an hour. We both admitted our fears that we had been suppressing–all of them. Our fears were similar, but I've come to realize that everyone's fears are similar when it comes down to it. We all fear losing our minds, probably more than losing our physical bodies. We fear losing our memories, especially those we cherish the most. We fear getting to the point where we don't recognize or remember those we love. We fear losing ourselves individually, and we fear losing us collectively. We fear the unknown, which life continually brings.

One of the greatest fears is losing control, but I've discovered something about that in my many years of life. Being in control is only an illusion. My theory is that we begin to subconsciously realize this as toddlers, which I believe to be the root of most of the "terrible two" tantrums. Even then, we are fighting for control. Then, as teenagers, we fight for independence from our parents. We want to control our own decisions and our own destinies, as if a person could ever fully control those things. Then, as an adult, we fight for control in every major area of life: love, career, finances, faith, and health. We try to play God, but lack the wisdom and the power. It is only through that struggle that we realize we *aren't* in control. All of the money, technology, and material things in the world that give us the temporary feeling of being in charge can be ripped away at a moment's notice. One major life change can take all of our money. People get sick without warning. People die unexpectedly.

People lose pieces of themselves, either by giving those pieces away or by having them taken away.

That has become my daily struggle: fighting for the pieces of me. Fighting for the pieces of my mind, which the fingers of my disease are slowly effacing, subtly lulling out one by one. Sometimes I am aware a piece is being taken, and I want to shout, "Hey! Don't take that one! I need that one!" only to feel like I am chasing down a taxi cab that is steadily pulling away from me. Other times, I don't realize a piece of me has been taken until I try to recall something that I know once was in there, but no longer can be reached. The piece is simply...gone.

And so I lie here with the pieces I have left. The pieces I cling to that are falling through my fingers like sand. At this point, I am still self-aware enough to realize this, and thus I feel a powerful inner prompting to do something about it...before all of the pieces are gone. Before I completely lose the battle.

And so I write this letter to you, my love. A letter telling you all of the things I feel deeply so that when all of the pieces of me are truly gone, you can read this letter over and over to remind yourself of what we have and that our love is still real, even if I can't reciprocate it any longer. Part of me hopes that it will be like *The Notebook*, where Noah reads to his Alzheimer-ridden love Allie and she occasionally comes back to him mentally, but the realist in me doesn't dare hope for that. That's book magic, which unfortunately doesn't often translate into the real world of mind-crippling diseases. So here goes. No magic. Just truth:

My Soulmate Ronnie,

You are mine and I am yours. Forever. Intertwined. Enmeshed. Two become one. Even when I am gone mentally and physically, know that I am still yours and am a part of you. Read this letter over and over again in the years to come and know that my love for you has never wavered or faded. Our love is still real, even when I can't express it any longer.

Ronnie and Ruby. It has always had a certain ring to it, hasn't it? I know this sounds silly, but growing up, I always wanted to marry a man whose name went well with mine. My parents, as you know, are named Matthew and Melody, and I always loved how their names sounded together. I know that's a ridiculous thing to want in a spouse, but nonetheless, it was on my "list" of future husband attributes. I even have it written in my teenage diary (which I have still kept to this day). I had made a list of names that go well with Ruby, and though Ronnie wasn't on the list (it would have been nestled alongside Rudy, Ralphie, and Raymond), I think it is a perfect match.

I remember meeting you at that wedding dance for a mutual family friend. If you recall (and my brain is recalling things well at the moment, so I need to go with it while I have it), the wedding dance was held in that enormous barn with the bottom cleaned out for dinner tables and the top cleared out for wedding dances. I had on my best dress, a dark green one that you later commented looked "purty" with my red hair, and I was ready for dancing. My sister and I sat on one of the side hay bales, our feet keeping time with the music, checking out all of the eligible young men, and suddenly you came into my line of vision. Oh, you were handsome in your navy suit and checkered red and white bow tie. You were hanging out with a few of your chums, and as you scanned the room (most likely looking for good-looking ladies), you caught me looking at you. I blushed instantly and looked down, too embarrassed to look up for a while, and suddenly you were in front of me asking if I wanted to dance. I almost couldn't speak, but I managed to nod my head, giving my sister a small smile as you took me out on the dance floor. We danced all night, and from then on, it was "Ronnie and Ruby" forever. I am glad you made the first move, or I might have just been looking down at my shoes all night.

From the moment I met you, I pictured growing old with you. At the time, it seemed like "growing old" would never happen to us, as we were young and naive about the ways of time. Even twenty seemed old to me when I graduated high school. Now, looking back, I don't know where all of the time has gone. We were teenagers in love and now we are the "cute old couple" that all of the young people point out and secretly want to emulate. As a teenager, I distinctly recall an older couple from my church, the Stenbergs, who always sat a few rows ahead of my family. I always looked for them every Sunday and inwardly admired them, though I never said more than "hello" at greeting time to them. Prior to church starting, they always walked down the church aisle hand in hand, smiling at everyone, joyfully content with each other and life. During the service, they stood together, arms around each other's shoulders, singing their heartfelt praises to God. As they grew older, Mrs. Stenberg's back began to arch, making her somewhat of a hunchback, but her husband never seemed to notice or mind. He still looked at her with utter adoration and devotion, a twinkle in his blue eyes as he gazed at his princess. She returned his affection with a doting smile that spoke volumes about their love for each other. Every time I saw them, it gave me hope for my future love. One Sunday, the Stenbergs weren't at church. I felt somewhat alarmed, as they were at church every week without fail, and asked my mother about it. She said that the pastor had told her that they died together in their sleep. I felt an immense sense of loss, wanting to smile and cry at the same time at the thought of the two holding each other all of the way into the afterlife. Shortly after that, I met you, and years melted into each other, and now we are the Stenbergs. Minus the hunchback.

I have so much to say, yet so little to say at the same time. You already know how I feel because I tell you every day: I love you. When I was young, a family friend of ours lost her husband in an auto accident, and the thing she kept repeating over and over again was, "I never told him I loved him before he left. I just nagged him about the mess in his office. I wish I would have told him that I loved him *instead." That profoundly affected me in ways I can't express, which is why I have always told you that I loved you before you left to go anywhere or before we got off the phone together. I just didn't want to miss that opportunity if it happened to be our last. I didn't want any regrets, and I am happy to say that I don't have any with you. The only thing that saddens me is the thought of leaving you mentally and eventually physically. I know at some point that it is going to be harder for you than for me, which is why I have to tell you that I love you while I am still mentally able. I love you more than a field of sunflowers with their "eyes" to the sun. More than a luminous rainbow on a rainy day. More than the feeling of sand beneath my toes at a beautiful beach. More than chocolate. (That one didn't need any extra explanation, since you know how much I love chocolate.)*

Besides expressing my deep-rooted love for you, I want to remind you to never forget the little things. Don't forget how we met. Don't forget our wedding day, mishaps and all. Don't forget the feeling of holding my hand, especially all of the times I cried during a sad movie. Don't forget to have faith in God and people. Don't forget that love is the most powerful force on the planet. Just...don't forget. Because I am starting to forget, and that is worse than the thought of death itself. I want to remember everything, but it appears that I don't have a choice in the matter.

Read this often and feel my love for you. Feel it like a chocolate chip cookie right out of the oven. Feel it like the slight breeze on a hot day. Feel it like the warmth of the sunshine after the clouds clear in the sky. Look up to the sky and feel my love all the way from heaven when I am gone. Remember that real love never dies. You can always feel it.

Forever Yours,

Ruby

Chapter 7

Robert

People have told me that I have the "artist's eye," the ability to take a picture at just the right angle, the best vantage point, to truly capture the magnitude–or "simplitude," as I am known for saying–of the subject matter. My younger sister, Flora, tells me that some of my photographs "wreck" her in a way she can't ever hope to explain. I've tried to get her to put it into words, this moment of destruction that I apparently do to her. One time, after a trip to Haiti to capture the damage of a recent hurricane, I sat on Flora's screened-in porch showing her photographs of my trip. She had only viewed a third of my pictures when a solitary tear escaped from the corner of her eye and made its way down her olive-toned cheek. In frustration, she quickly wiped the tear from her face and sighed impatiently.

"What is it?" I had asked, my brown eyes boring inquisitively into hers.

"Oh, you've done it again. Wrecked me," she replied irritatedly.

As any good brother would do, I laughed out loud at her obvious discomfort. "Well, shouldn't pictures move people? Isn't that the *point* of taking them?" I countered, leaning back in my chair and running my fingers through my dark hair on both sides in mock frustration.

She gave me that squinty-eyed look that only sisters can give when they are truly annoyed with their brothers. I believe I used to call it the "stink eye" when we were young. "Yes, but...but-"

"But what?" I said, tilting my head and lowering my voice, trying to ease out of her what she had been trying to tell me for years.

She sighed and threw up her hands. "Why even try to explain it to you? I never can seem to find the words for it."

Despite her obvious frustration, I really did want to know what she was trying to say. I reached for her hand and asked softly, "Please try, Flora. I want to know."

She looked out the window, attempting to gather her thoughts into coherent words. "Well, I guess the only way that I can explain it is that you capture the absolute horrors and evils of life so clearly that it just rips a person apart. Right here," she paused to put my hand on her heart and continued, "in the heart. It pierces straight through. But then, you also include a hint of beauty, as to give the viewer a taste of hope, and that puts a person back together again."

She then looked down at the last picture she had viewed. "Like this photograph. You have this sweet child who couldn't be more than five years old, rummaging through this garbage heap, and that just tears a person apart to think about all of the loss that child has undergone. Her house is destroyed. Her family. Everything. Just wiped out in a single moment."

She paused as another tear rolled down her cheek. "But then, in the corner of all of that rubble, there is a yellow flower in full bloom, perfectly radiant and stunning, reminding a person that even in the midst of tragedy, there is beauty from the ashes, so to speak." She looked up and looked straight into my eyes. "Every picture is the constant ripping apart and stitching back together of one's heart. And a person can only take so much of that." She sighed. "THAT is why I can only see a portion of your photographs every time. The human heart can only handle so much."

We both sat in silence as I pondered her words. "So it's the juxtaposition of the horrors and beauty of this life in my photographs that tears a person apart? That is what you are saying?"

She laughed. "Well, that's a fancy photojournalist way of putting it, yes, but I think it's more fitting to call it the inner wrecking of a person."

She looked me in the eye, her hand still holding mine. "You've always had a knack for taking pictures, ever since you were a child. Remember when you used to 'borrow' mom's camera when she wasn't looking and take as many pictures as you could before she noticed? She would be looking through her pictures later and comment how she simply couldn't delete your pictures, even if you were only five at the time, because they were better than the ones she took."

I smiled at the memory. "Yeah, it got to the point where she would delete her own pictures and leave all of mine."

Flora's brown eyes crinkled at the corners as a reminiscent smile formed on her face. "And THEN she got smart and realized that she could just hand you the camera and ask you to take pictures. She didn't even attempt to take her own pictures after that. That's when you became the family photographer." She paused, reflecting on the memory. "Now you're the WORLD photographer. Sometimes I just can't believe it."

"To be honest, sometimes I can't believe it, either," I admitted.

She cleared her throat and looked out the window, as if deep in thought. "Yes, you've always been good at what you do. But, lately, ever since..." she paused, looking for the right words, "...the accident, your pictures have had the ability to wreck me even more. I feel it more than I used to. Your pictures *say* more than they used to."

I looked away. The accident. Still so hard to talk about or even think about. I knew that my ability to capture both the pain and the beauty of life was refined by fire–the fire that came when a drunk driver hit the car that held my wife and daughter head-on and the car erupted into flame before the police or fire department were able to perform a rescue. The fire ignited that night two years ago still raged within me, the tongues of flame driving me onward, ready to devour me if I ever slowed down enough to let my guard down.

Yes, perhaps I do have the artistic eye for the camera, but it didn't come easily for me. I had to learn this "inner wrecking," this ability to see beauty in the midst of agony, for myself before I was able to perfectly capture it in my photographs. Such is the great irony of life: To gain wisdom a person's heart has to be refined by fire, but our hearts don't want to experience the pain that comes from the heat. I would rather have remained a moderately successful photojournalist with the lives of my wife and daughter intact rather than be the highly sought-after photojournalist with the empty house that I am today. It seems that fate didn't ask my opinion on the matter.

Yes, my pictures kept me going when I was at my lowest point and continue to keep me from the brink of despair. They have given me a purpose where I have felt lost the past few years. Through my lens, I see my wife and daughter alive again, living on in the people and things that I photograph. Every time I capture a woman's smile, I see my wife's easy smile warming my heart on the other side of the lens and think, *Lenora, I miss you.*

Every time I capture a sweet child's face, I feel the innocence of my daughter, Anna, speaking to my very soul. I remember holding Anna's sweet hand as she looked up adoringly at me with her big, brown eyes that said, *Daddy, I think you can do anything*. Every time I capture something beautiful in nature, I remember a place we used to go as a family that nurtured my inner being. I see them in everything I capture through my lens, and it makes me strive to get the perfect angle, the perfect vantage point, to accurately portray the message they are trying to convey. *That* is why my pictures have increased in quality since the accident. My loves, the mother and daughter team of my universe, speak to me through the camera and their stories need to be shared with others.

And share them I have. My pictures have been on the cover over multiple magazines, including *National Geographic* and *Time Magazine*. I was named "Photojournalist of the Year" this past year and attended a gala event that displayed many of my photographs, primarily from the past two years. People who attended this event couldn't wait to meet the man who "touched their inner being" with his pictures. One woman had tears running down her cheeks as she explained how a picture and story about a child saved from the rubble of a recent earthquake had warmed her heart and compelled her to donate a large sum of money to the organizations and charities involved with cleaning up the damage.

Yet no amount of fame or accolades will ever bring them back, and that is the truth I have to live with on a daily basis. I miss them in ways I can't even begin to explain in words. The vast loneliness that I feel when I come home to an empty house that has reminders of them in every nook and cranny, every crevice, cannot be ignored. When I stare at my face in the mirror–my dark skin etched with the deep lines of grief–I feel like a stranger is looking back at me, a ghost of the man I used to be.

My only living solace is my yellow lab, Lucky, who is true to his name because he was the sole survivor of the crash. Lenora and Anna had been enroute with Lucky to the vet when the accident happened. Lucky was injured, but relatively unscathed from the whole incident, which seemed impossible based on the wretched condition of the car. Lucky was perhaps the only thing that got me out of bed in the mornings immediately following the accident because something was *depending* on me for life. If it wasn't for that dog, I might have spent the first two weeks after the accident entirely in bed. Lucky saved me, in a way. He has been a good companion, even if he is a mischievous little devil at times. Ironically, the chewed-up cords and slippers that used to continually annoy me have now become a source of humor and purpose in my otherwise cheerless life.

This may sound strange, but something else that has kept me sane has been keeping scrapbooks for Lenora and Anna. When I take a picture of someone or something that reminds me of either one of them, I develop the photograph and stick it in the scrapbook with a short paragraph describing when and where I took the picture and why it reminded me of one of "my girls," as I used to call them. In a way, it is a form of catharsis for me; a way of coping with their deaths while keeping their memories alive. I never want to forget how Lenora's blue eyes would widen at the mention of flowers of any kind or how Anna loved every one of God's creatures, even the slimy ones from the ground like slugs and worms. With pictures I can remember and celebrate those things. I feel close to them every time I carefully place a new photograph in the sleeve and lovingly write about how the picture reminded me of them. I take pictures to remember the things I never want to forget.

That's the thing about pictures. They can transport you to a certain place, a specific time; they are portals to the senses that evoke our memories. A picture of bread can transport me to a memory of Lenora baking a fresh loaf in our kitchen, the smells wafting through the house and out the front door as I enter, the three of us breaking warm bread together around the dinner table. A picture of a worm in the dirt can bring me back to digging with a trowel in the backyard with Anna, and I can almost hear her ecstatic squeal every time we found a new worm for her to put in her worm box, her sweet giggles music to my soul. A picture of a white daisy transports me to the field by our house that is filled with daisies every summer, and I can see both of my girls weaving daisy chains and placing them atop their heads, princesses in Daisyland, as they used to call it. A picture is worth a thousand words, as they say, even if I can't help wishing my photographs had the power to bring back the dead in actuality rather than just memory.

Until the day I see them again, I will keep on taking pictures for their scrapbooks in remembrance of the joy and light they brought to my life. It's my love letter to them and I will keep on clicking away at the camera and writing my love notes underneath. It might seem silly, but a part of me envisions that they can somehow look down from where they are and see the entries that I write for them. I sometimes read the caption that I have written underneath each picture aloud, as if Lenora and Anna were physically somewhere nearby and I were sharing the photograph and memory with them. Here are a few entries from the past year:

Lucky may be getting older, but he's always ready to play in the leaves with you, Anna. Remember how you both used to love playing in the crisp autumn leaves? Mom and I would help you rake the yard, you with your little pink rake, and when the pile was deemed "big enough," you and Lucky would charge in and jump, your giggles and

Lucky's happy barks shaking the leaf pile from within after you were enveloped in autumnal bliss.

I remember one such perfect fall day a few months before the accident when the fall sunshine was flitting through the trees and we were all outside in our light jackets and caps, our cheeks pink from the chill of the day. You and Lucky were jumping in the "biggest pile EVER," or so you stated, and I had stuck my head in the leaf pile to check on you because you had been in there so long. What I found was you with your eyes closed, a huge smile on your face. Without opening your eyes, you said, "Listen, Daddy! Do you hear them?" Confused, I had asked who you meant, and you answered, "The autumn fairies, of course! You can hear their wings humming if you close your eyes and listen."

I raked a pile of leaves the other day in remembrance of you, and I sat with Lucky with my eyes closed, listening for the fairies. The funny thing is that I swore I could hear their wings just above the whisper of the wind. You were right, Anna. I hope you can see the fairies all around you where you are now.

The maple across the pond was magnificent this past fall, Lenora. When we used to go for one of our evening walks, you would often stop and stare at the "majestic maple," as if transfixing its beauty permanently into your memory. You commented about how "beauty is fleeting," like the sunset, where the palette of fiery colors is at its peak for only a short time, but those moments leave a person breathless with wonder.

I remember how it saddened you when the tree shed all of its leaves every year. Once, I saw a tear fall down your cheek as you slowed your pace and looked mournfully at the tree. When I asked you what was wrong, you said, "I have to wait an entire year before I see its loveliness again." I recalled this moment after the accident because I felt the same way. Your intense beauty, the way you lit up this world with an array of gorgeous colors, was suddenly gone and I felt its absence with a ferocity that was palpable. Now I am the one who stares at the tree after it has dropped its final leaf and I think, "I have to wait a lifetime before I see Lenora's beauty again."

In your honor, I planted a sugar maple tree in our yard this past year because it makes me think of you. How you would have loved seeing its blaze of colors every fall. I await the day that I will see your beauty emblazon my gaze, Lenora. Until then...

Don't worry, girls, Maggie the Mad Hopper is still going strong and is as soft as ever. She misses her daily petting from you two, though. (She told me with a twitch of her nose.) I picked clover for her all summer from our field so she would have fresh greens for breakfast, just like you two used to do every day. I have been letting her run around in her pen in the grass as often as possible, and she still is up to her old tricks where she runs around in circles in order to evade me when it's time to go back to her main cage. You both used to laugh whenever she did that, leading to her nickname of "Maggie the Mad Hopper" that she is still earning on a daily basis. She says "hi" with another twitch of her nose, by the way.

Sea glass! Your favorite, Lenora. As you always used to say, "The sea is calling," and it has continued to do so, even after you were gone. As they have done in previous years, Tom and Tammy invited me to their lake cabin multiple times this summer. Though it wasn't the same without you two there, the sand in my toes and sea wind in my hair performed their magic on me once again as I searched for sea glass for our collection at home. Last weekend, I found a green and a blue piece of glass, which were your favorite two colors because they were so rare. The sea reminds me of you, and when I walk along the shore, I swear I can almost hear your soft voice and Anna's sweet giggles riding on the waves, traveling over time and space to help me feel close to you. I still have the necklace I made you, the one with the hole cut through a piece of sky blue sea glass, the one you wore faithfully every day until the ac-

cident stole you away from me. Your necklace and wedding ring were two of the only things recovered from the wreckage, and I slipped your ring onto the necklace with the blue sea glass so I could hang it in the office window at home to remind me of you every day. That, along with our family vase of sea glass, continually remind me of the many hours we have spent together searching for the beauty that I have realized was already all around us.

The neighbors, the Sands, recently acquired a goat named Annabel. This is how I met Annabel—at our mailbox eating a section of the newspaper that HAD been in our box—as the Sands apologized profusely. Since I only had my phone on me and not my camera, I snapped a quick picture because I knew that you and Anna would find it hilarious. I learned (after their apologies that I had dismissed with a laugh and a wave of my hand) that Annabel is a Pygmy goat that the neighbors plan on showing at the county fair coming up. They told me that they hoped they could teach her some better manners because

she eats EVERYTHING in sight...including our newspaper, apparently.

Anna, I remember how the goat section at the fair was always your favorite, ever since you were a toddler. I recall the time when you were just shy of two years old and you kept saying "go" at home. It wasn't until we went to the county fair for the second time that week that we realized you were saying "goAT" instead of "go," and we laughed until tears streamed down our cheeks. You pointed at every goat, especially the little ones, and said, "Go!" excitedly, until it dawned on us what you had been trying to tell us at home.

I went to the fair last summer, my first summer without my girls, and I visited the goat section first in remembrance of you. I could almost hear your sweet little voice saying "go" at every goat. I will be sure to visit Annabel the pygmy goat when I go to the upcoming fair and pet her for you, sweet girl.

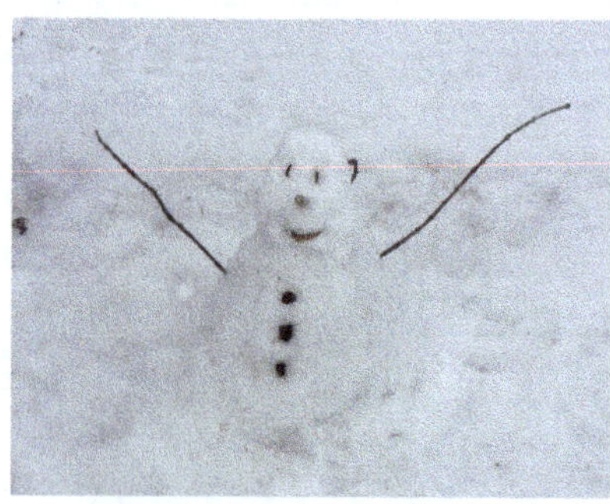

Do you want to build a snowman? Look how small this snowman is, Anna. I really needed help from my two girls

to make it bigger. Even though it was a sad attempt on my part, I make sure I build at least one snowman every winter in honor of you. I remember how you always wanted to build snow people AND their pets, so we ended up building many snow dogs and snow cats along the way.

This past winter, I went to an ice and snow sculpting display and was amazed. I had trouble believing that they cut the ice with chainsaws, but I witnessed it with my own two eyes. There were sculptures of all kinds—animals from around the world, an ice palace that you would have LOVED to live in with the winter fairies, and even a dragon scene that looked like a person could just jump on the back and fly away into the blue beyond. Then, just past the ice sculpting section, there was a snow crafting section. The builders called themselves the "snow masters," and masters they were. My favorite snow structure was an enormous pirate ship that took one whole week to build, according to the sign. The snow masters had a snow pirate at the helm, complete with a patch over his eye, and it was the patch that made me want to yell out, "Aye, Matey!" like we used to do at home when we were playing pirates. I bet we could have become snow masters with a few more years of practice, Anna.

Christmas. The time I miss my girls the most. The first Christmas immediately following the accident, I didn't have the heart to pull out the homemade ornaments. I did finally get a tree, but the only decoration on the tree was the lights. I just didn't have the heart to put up all the ornaments that represented our life together.

This past Christmas, I took things one day at a time. A few weeks before Christmas, I went to Olson's Tree Farm and picked out the "perfect tree," as you used to call it, Anna. It was a foot taller than I am, about seven feet, with full branches that would hold a multitude of ornaments. It smelled of pine and the outdoors. I cut it down, paid for it, brought it home, and put it up. Well, more accurately, I attempted to put it up. I realized at that moment that Christmas trees weren't meant to be put up by a single person. When I was lugging the tree in the front door, I really missed my "door holder," as you used to call yourself, Anna, because the cold north wind kept blowing the door shut on me and the tree. After I finally manhandled the tree inside, the wind slamming the front door on my back-

side as I made the last push inside, I sat down to take a breather and wished you were here, Lenora, to help carry one end of the tree. I lost count of the number of walls and furniture that I hit with the tip of the tree before I made it to the large living room window facing the road, where we always put up the tree. I needed to sit on the couch for another breather before I attempted to stand the tree up in the tree stand, which is the point where I really needed my girls. Trying to straighten a tree AND adjust the tree stand without another person to say "a smidge left" or "a little more to the right" took three times as long, and, to be honest, the tree still looks a bit crooked to me. I'm sure, if you are able to look down from where you are, you both laughed until tears streamed down your face.

Anyway, getting the tree and attempting to put it up was day one. Day two, I came home from work and put the lights on the tree. I missed my Super Light Untangler, Anna. After about twenty minutes of detangling, I started winding the lights around the tree, but you were always the best at spacing the lights, Lenora. I had the lights bunched in one spot and completely lacking in another. I attempted to fix it, but I'm pretty sure I made it worse.

Day three (this is sounding somewhat like the Creation Story, though I definitely didn't have any divine intervention) I took the Christmas decorations out of the closet, but I didn't actually get any of them on the tree. I just opened the bins and remembered. Every decoration, every ornament, had a memory tied to it. The garland that we put up the bannister going up the stairs made me remem-

ber how Lucky tore it down three times when he was a puppy. You were so mad at him, Lenora. I actually thought you might give him away after the garland came down for the third time. Anna pleaded with you, saying, "It's not Lucky's fault, Mama. He's just a playful little puppy." In another bin, I found the Christmas bell, which Anna loved to ring for dinner every night to signal that we all "find our places at the table." I remember how vigorously Anna rang that bell every meal. I think we came to the table faster than usual because we wanted the cacophonous ringing to cease.

Day four I mustered my inner Christmas spirit and put some of the ornaments on the tree. I say "some" because I was only able to hang about a third of them before I missed my girls so much that I couldn't add any more. The ornament that really got to me—the one in the picture above—made me remember how you girls made multiple ornaments for gifts, with Mommy painting and Anna cutting the hanging ribbon for each one. Anna, you told me that the buffalo plaid was a good "dad pattern" and kept one to give to me for a gift, explaining that the word "merry" was a reminder of how I always needed to be around Christmastime. When I took this ornament out of the box and the memories of that day came flooding back, I noticed a little crack had appeared right below the ribbon. It matched how I felt—I was trying to be merry, but life had put a crack in it and the usual Christmas cheer could not fully permeate its way to my heart. I have vowed to be as cheerful as possible without you here, which is the best

I can do for now. I even put a little Santa hat on Lucky to help foster more Christmas spirit, and I think it is working.

Merry Christmas, my loves!

Chapter 8

Lily

A beautiful flower. That's me all right. At least in theory. The thing about a flower is that it has a short period of blooming where the colors are gorgeously displayed–and then it wilts. The colors fade. The petals shrink and fall off. They dry up and are discarded or forgotten. That's how I feel. I bloomed and now have wilted.

The thing is that I used to feel like the beautiful flower for which I am named. When I was young, the world seemed fresh and new, full of promise and adventure around every corner. Those were the days when my mom and dad told me that they loved me every day and would remind me that I was special and beautiful, like the lily flower. In fact, that became their nickname for me: Lily Flower. Whenever I did something that they found especially cute or amusing, they would say,

"Oh, my sweet Lily Flower" or some variation of that phrase. Yes, those were the days of enchantment. Now the magic seemingly has worn off.

Those were the days when my mom and dad got along, but that world seems so far away now. When I was six, my father took a different job that made more money but was very demanding of his time and energy. For one, he had an hour commute and had to get up by 5:00 and leave by 6:00. The sweet mornings of snuggling and eating breakfast together were gone. When I woke up, he had typically already left for work. We used to eat dinner together as a family every night, but the demands of the new job often brought him home after dinner, much to my disappointment and my mother's annoyance.

This is when the fighting began and the beauty and enchantment of the world began to fade. The "Lily Flower" began wilting, on the inside first and then outwardly. They initially tried to hide their fights from me, quarreling in hushed tones behind closed doors, but then the arguments became more explosive and couldn't be hidden any longer. My father started staying even later at work, which made my mother even more angry. Then something happened. Something big. I could feel it. They never told me what it was, but I just know that things were never the same after that. I used to hope that they would stop fighting and would go back to how they used to be, back to our loving family, but whatever big thing that had happened seemed to be the point of no return. The two of them stopped arguing, but they also stopped talking to each other altogether, which was even worse. The silence in the house was unbearable. My father moved into a different bedroom for a few months, and then one day he was just gone. He went to work and never came back home.

He never even said goodbye to me. I was usually sleeping when he left, but for some reason, I couldn't sleep that night and was wide awake in the morning. My door was open, and when my father walked by to leave for work, he stopped and looked at me, still lying in my bed. Our eyes met, but there was a vacant expression on his face. He stared at me for a moment, and then he was gone. Just like that. I could sense that something was off, so I got out of bed and ran to my window. I watched him walk out to the car and drive away. He never came back.

I replay that scene over and over again in my mind. Why couldn't he have said a proper goodbye? Why didn't he come into my room and hold me just one last time? Why couldn't he have whispered, "I will always love you, my Lily Flower" one last time, just like he used to do, before he left? I feel like that would have made all of the difference. There would have at least been some closure for me. The way it happened left me feeling abandoned. Discarded. Unimportant. Hurt. Angry.

The weird thing is that my mother never even addressed what happened. It was like she almost expected that it was going to happen, and then when it did, she didn't feel the need to talk about it. It was like she wanted to pretend that he had never existed. Maybe it was easier for her that way. She took down all of the pictures that had him in it, which was nearly all of the ones we had. She didn't bother replacing them with other pictures, so our house just felt impersonal and bare after that. It was like one of those houses that was staged before it was to be sold, stripped of anything that made it personal and made to look like anyone could move in. The thing about looking like *anyone* could move in is that it doesn't feel like a home any longer to the people who actually live there. Usually a house becomes a home for people, but in this case, our home converted back into just a house. A house where two people lived side by side but didn't act like a family any longer.

My mother then became what I would call a "functional mother," just like when some people are "functional alcoholics" and can still make the decisions and actions that make life work. She went to work every day. She went grocery shopping and made meals. She drove me to the places I needed to go. She did laundry. But she did it all with very few words. And certainly no love was expressed in any of it. No hugs. No kisses. No "I love you's" were spoken. In fact, I didn't recall either parent expressing they loved me at any point after the fighting turned ugly. It was as if the love was squeezed out from our house, much like a piece of fruit that has been juiced and only the outer shell is left.

A mother's gentle touch. That is what I have missed the most. She used to be so tender with me when I was younger, cupping my face in her hand or putting a stray hair behind my ear. She would always hold the touch for just a moment and look me straight in the eye and say, "I love you, my Lily Flower." At night, if I were sick, she would stay with me until I fell asleep, gently stroking my hair. I miss that part of my mom. The gentle mom. The mom of my past who haunts my present because she made me acutely aware of what I am now missing.

It makes me wonder, *Is she not capable of showing love any longer because she feels unloved?* At first I thought she might not be capable of *actual love* any longer, but in my heart of hearts, I feel that can't be true for anyone. I am not a cynic. Perhaps she just can't *show it* any more because of what happened with my dad, whatever that was.

Maybe it dried up her heart in some way. Perhaps her heart is like a seed that the wind has blown from a flower after the summer has ended, tossed and turned and dried out, finally landing somewhere far away. The seasons have changed from autumn to winter, and the seed has been covered with a thick, white blanket of snow. The winter has grown colder. Bitter-cold. Barren. Forlorn. Hopeless at times. Maybe the seed wonders if it will ever feel warmth and produce life again. Maybe it feels like it can't any longer.

But here is what I tell myself to get through the tough days, since there are a lot of them: Seasons change. Slowly sometimes, but they do eventually change. Ultimately, even in the coldest climates, spring comes, bringing the long-awaited sunshine and warmth to the world, letting that tiny, hardened little seed find life again. This is what I cling to for myself (the wilted Lily Flower) and for my mother (the hardened seed). I can still pray and hope for spring to come for our household.

I refuse to become embittered. I see what bitterness has done to both of my parents, and I want no part of that. I will choose hope over fear. I have seen goodness and love in this world, first in my parents when I was young and after in acts of kindness from people all around me.

One of the people who has extended kindness to me has been my art teacher at school, Mrs. Clay. I always thought her name was so fitting, since we often work with clay during our pottery units in class. Mrs. Clay always has a smile on her face and a kind word on her lips for every person in the room. She is passionate about the transformative power of art and tells us all about it while we are working. She makes her way around the art room, like a hummingbird flitting from flower to flower, saying things like, "Let your art say what your lips cannot!" and "Never forget that art brings hope and light into this dark world!" or, my personal favorite, "Art turns your wounds into light!"

Art turns wounds into light. I mulled that sentiment over and over again in my brain, like a cow chewing its cud, while I worked on my most recent painting. Creating art had truly become an outlet for me, but I had never fully contemplated *why* until Mrs. Clay said that statement aloud. I realized that my teacher had captured in words what art was doing for me all along: It was turning my inner wounds into beauty and light on canvas. I stopped painting for a moment and tilted my head, deep in thought, as I considered the subject matter of my painting. A large, pink lily was stretching its blossom towards the light of the sun, soaking up the warmth of the luxuriant rays. I saw myself in that flower, seeking the warmth and light from above. *I will bloom again*, I thought determinedly as I looked at the blended colors depicting the sun's rays.

As I put some of the finishing touches on my painting, I had an idea of what I could do with this particular piece of art. Besides hanging it in my bedroom, which had become a gallery of sorts, I could turn my artwork into something else. Recently, one of my friend's aunts, who owned a small art gallery in the city, showed us how her gallery's artists had turned their artwork prints into greeting cards that could be purchased in her store. Apparently, they had been selling like hotcakes, as many people who weren't willing to pay (or house) a large piece of artwork were more than willing to buy multiple greeting cards to send to family and friends. My friend, Amanda, commented to her Aunt Mallory that I was also an artist, and her eyes lit up, immediately interested in my artwork. After showing her a few pictures of my most recent pieces, Mallory invited me to turn my artwork into greeting cards for her gallery. I humbly declined at the time, as I didn't feel my artwork was in the same league as her gallery's artists, but she left it as an open invitation for the future. I hadn't really given it another thought until now.

What if I took Amanda's aunt up on her offer? *What if?* I knew those two simple words had launched a multitude of people's dreams throughout history, and I didn't want to limit myself by not asking them.

I made the decision then and there to contact Amanda's aunt and accept her gracious offer to make my artwork into a greeting card. I also decided who would be the first two recipients of my cards: my mom and my dad. I lived with my mom, so it wouldn't be difficult to leave it somewhere that she would easily find it. My father would be a different story. I would have to do some detective work to track down his whereabouts and address, but I was determined to make it happen. I began to formulate what I would say to each one. As I painted, I imagined the words in my cards going something like this:

My Tough-As-Nails Mother,

I want you to know that I admire you. I admire the strength that it must have taken to survive Dad leaving us. I marvel at the tenacity that it took to keep getting up, day after day, going to work to keep a roof over our heads and food on the table. I respect the way that you never gave up on me or on life.

How I envied your strength while I was growing up. Whereas I always felt one errant word or abstract thought away from a good cry, you continually seemed to be the pillar of strength that no person or circumstance could crumble. I continually wondered how you could appear so strong all of the time.

Though I admire that strength, I also need you to know that it's okay to not be strong all of the time. You are human. You don't have to put up a front for me. I know you've felt sad and overwhelmed, even if you haven't shown it to me. I want you to know that I can take it. In fact, I want you to share things with me. I miss seeing the tender side of you. I miss your hugs and kisses. I miss feeling like a team that can take on the world. Together.

Love Always,

Lily

And to my dad:

Dear Daddy,

How I've missed you. I have missed your laugh that seemed to emanate from your entire being when you thought something I did was funny. I have missed your loving, head-tilting smile when I did something you found endearing. I miss the kindness radiating from your brown eyes in the form of soft wrinkles (which you called "smile lines") when you talked with me. I miss the father-daughter "date nights" that we used to have before you left.

Why did you leave us, Dad? Why did you leave me? That is the question that has eaten away at my soul for years for which I am still desperate to hear your answer. I know that you and Mom weren't getting along, but when you left without a proper goodbye, it shattered my world. I felt lost, like a small boat getting tossed on the waves of uncertainty. Time has healed some of my wounds, but I still feel like that boat at times. Little girls need their daddies, and when you left, you robbed me of that inner feeling that everything would be all right. The waves of self-doubt continue to roll over me to this day. I wish you were here to quell the storm.

Through it all, I still love you and want to reconnect with you. You are still my daddy and I am still your little girl, and nothing will ever change that. It's not too late, Dad. I anxiously await your reply.

Always,

Your Lily-Flower

Chapter 9

Millie

Raspberries. I can't get enough of them. They are an alluring red, perfectly round and succulently sweet. In the morning dew, they dazzle the eyes as the rays of Aurora silently stretch across the horizon. They tantalize the taste buds with each and every bite, forcing the taster to savor the sweetness, as it only lasts a short while. Like I said, I'm just plain crazy for raspberries.

I have a little patch going. Well, that might be an understatement. It's not so little anymore. When my late husband, Henry, was alive, we decided to start a small patch in the field we owned behind our garden. We had a few raspberry shoots from a neighbor that he claimed were "the best raspberries on the planet." I remember being confused, as I thought all raspberries were pretty much the same, but he was right. Just like people, some raspberries are sweeter than others. Ours were the largest, reddest, sweetest raspberries that I have ever tasted. One taste was all it took. I was hooked for life.

Our small patch steadily grew as we replanted the new shoots every spring into additional rows. Soon, we had more raspberries than we knew what to do with. I made jams, jellies, pies, and other tasty treats. I snacked on them between meals. I ate them for dessert. I finally admitted to Henry that perhaps we had a raspberry problem. He threw his head back and laughed at me the way he always did when he found my antics especially amusing, and simply said, "It's not a problem. We just need to share them."

My eyes grew wide, slightly alarmed at the prospect of the entire neighborhood scouring our patch, when Henry, as if reading my mind, added, "Not with every-one, silly. Let's just start with the grandkids."

I smiled and nodded, and then I made a few phone calls. We had four children who were all married with families of their own, and all of them lived relatively close by us. We invited them all over for a weekend bar-becue and raspberry picking.

The next Saturday afternoon, following a barbecue lunch of ribs, chicken, corn on the cob, and, of course, an array of raspberry fruit salads and desserts, Henry and I sat the kids and grandkids down to talk business. They laughed at our seriousness when we said that we needed to talk about raspberries. After explaining how big our patch had grown and our need to have some extra pickers on hand, one of our brightest grandkids, Addie, asked if we could make a deal.

"What kind of a deal?" I had asked with a curious arched brow.

"A deal you can't pass up," Addie had explained excitedly. "How about we grandkids come and help you plant new shoots in the spring, weed the patch, and pick the raspberries in exchange for all of us being able to come and pick as many raspberries as we want for eating? Does that sound like a fair deal?"

I had looked at Henry and he had simply given me "the nod," which signified his agreement, so I said, "Deal!" and shook Addie's hand to seal the arrangement.

It was then that I took them behind the shed to the field where we had started our little patch. Their eyes grew wide. "Grandma and Grandpa! It's way bigger than it was last year! No wonder you wanted our help!"

Henry's eyes twinkled mischievously as he watched the grandkids take in the entirety of the patch. "Yep, we got a little desperate and had to recruit you munchkins. Now don't get lost in the raspberry patch! I don't want to go out to pick raspberries tomorrow and find one of my grandkids instead!"

The kids and grandkids had laughed and laughed at the prospect of finding someone amidst the raspberries, and that was the beginning of the "Raskob Raspberries" family business that we still own today.

Over the years, Henry and I slowed down somewhat, but the rest of the family compensated by being more than enough help during the busy season. They all take shifts at the booth where people can either choose a container to pick their own berries or buy pre-picked berries at a higher price, which is also where I annually set up shop with my baked goods: pies, jams, jellies, cookies, muffins, cakes, and other pastries. Sometimes, when it's hot outside, the grandkids insist on offering raspberry smoothies, which always goes over well with the customers.

Yes, it has developed into quite the little business. Our patch has grown to over thirty rows over the years, and our raspberries are widely known as the biggest, sweetest berries around. People drive from miles away every year just to stock up on our succulent treats, and they always comment that it's worth the drive. Some people alter their vacation routes to incorporate a pit stop at our berry patch. I can always tell who is on vacation, with the overloaded vehicles and their please-sell-us-something-that-will-make-our-car-ride-go-better demeanors. We know we have made a difference when we watch people bite into our raspberries or homemade goodies and smiles slowly spread across all of their faces.

Besides offering the most tasty treats around, we also try to add smiles to people's faces by adding quotes and words of wisdom on our "Raskob Raspberries" stickers that are placed on each purchase. I personally hand write them all while working in the booth every day, which keeps me busy between customers. Some are age-old adages that I have always liked, and some are made up by me. Before he passed, Henry liked to call them my "berry wise bits of wisdom" for the world. I'm sure that some people don't even notice them as they rush to eat their newly-purchased sweet treats, but I would venture that at least half of the customers pause for a moment to read and consider the words written on the stickers, and so I write my messages to the world–or at least the part of the world located within a certain radius of my raspberry patch. As I've gotten older, I have more fully realized the benefits of wisdom and see a shortage of it in this world, both amongst the young and the old. Age doesn't necessarily bring wisdom; it simply brings experiences and lessons through which we can glean wisdom if we are receptive and willing to listen. I feel a need to share the wisdom that I have gathered from life with anyone who is willing to incline a listening ear. Anyway, here are just some of the "bits" that I have come up with over the years...

Millie's "Berry Wise" Bits of Wisdom:

Save your life by spending it on the people who
mean the most to you.
- Millie

Every time you blink, another moment has passed
before your eyes.
Make the next blink count.
- Millie

There's no U-Haul behind the hearse.
- Millie

Material things are the big distraction.
Don't get too distracted or you'll end up with lots of
stuff
and no one around to share it with you.
- Millie

It is wise to look before you leap in life,
but just make sure you LEAP!"
- Millie

You come into this life with nothing;
you go out with nothing but the memories you have
made
and the wisdom that you have learned."
- Millie

Curiosity may have killed the cat,
but at least it went out of life learning something.
- Millie

It may be *hard* to teach an old dog new tricks,
but dogs are never too old to learn something new.
- Millie

Don't judge a book by its cover,
but also realize the cover is the book's first impres-
sion.
- Millie

Let us all eat cake.
It's delicious!
- Millie

The best things in life are freely given
and freely accepted.
- Millie

Never lose the ability to wonder like a child.
Wondering piques the imagination.
- Millie

Many hands make light work,
But many hard-working hands
make even lighter work.
- Millie

Learn to be content in all stages of life.
Each situation has something to teach you
only IF you are willing to listen.
- Millie

Enjoy!
Not just this raspberry,
but each raspberry and every MOMENT.
- Millie

(Henry wanted to add one, and this was the one he
came up with before he passed,
given that he was the night owl in the family:)

The early bird may catch the worm, but the night
owl gets the remote all to himself.
- Henry

Chapter 10

Chen

I have two words for you: toilet paper. Who knew that toilet paper is what people would hoard during the virus? I recently saw a meme where a guy was running through a warzone with toilet paper clenched to his chest, bombs going off left and right. Though the video made me laugh out loud, the reality of the virus has been no laughing matter—a warzone for our country and our world.

I am a Chinese-American, born in this country with pride. My grandparents immigrated to the United States from China in the 1970s, hoping for better business opportunities and a less-crowded life for their children. They moved to California, since there is a large Chinese population there and the weather is pleasant year-round. My grandfather started his own business, a shoe store called Happy Soles, somewhat near the beach, which he passed down to my father when the time seemed right. That shoe shop has been our family's livelihood for two (going on three) generations and our source of a livable income. Until lately.

How people react to hardship is mystifying to me. When the virus first came to California, some people were scared, but business went on as usual. Customers came in, some with a certain shoe in mind and others browsing until a pair struck their fancy. Then, as the virus began to spread, I began to notice a change in people. The foot traffic began to lessen, and some of our customers stopped looking us in the eye when buying shoes. It was the most bizarre thing. Some of our most loyal customers started acting like...strangers. Then people simply stopped coming. It wasn't just my family's shoe store, but any establishment that had someone who looked like an ounce of Chinese blood was coursing through the veins. People were still out shopping and going to restaurants, just not to *our* shops and dining establishments.

Then came the backlash. The xenophobia. Not from everyone, but from enough people to make it hurtful. Once, while riding the bus from our house to our store, my father coughed because he had something caught in his throat. A man close to him gave him a scathing look and said, "Go back to your own country!" and cursed at my father for "not covering his cough." Plenty of other people had coughed on the bus prior to that, but my father and I were the only two who looked Chinese enough to elicit the tonguelashing. I wanted to excuse the man's behavior, to pass it off as a stress-induced comment due to the recent rise in anxiety from the virus, but I couldn't. In my heart of hearts, there is no excuse for treating someone that way, especially an older gentleman like my father.

Prior to the virus, I had noticed racial tensions in our country but had never personally been on the receiving end. I had never taken the brunt of hateful comments, and it surprised me—no, *shocked* me would be more accurate—when it started happening. It wasn't even logical. I was just like any other American worker, going to and from my place of employment, providing for my family. None of my family members had been out of the country for years because we were so busy working. How did "looking" Chinese give us a greater probability for passing on the virus? The answer is it didn't, but that didn't stop people from jumping to conclusions.

Given our location, we have an ethnically diverse population. Prior to the virus closing our doors for the state "lockdown," one of our customers, Mr. Malcolm, was browsing for shoes, which happened pretty often because he had somewhat of a shoe fetish. He had an entire walk-in closet just for his shoes, which I know because he told me multiple times. I couldn't even imagine owning that many pairs of shoes for my personal collection. Though my family owned a shoe store, my grandparents and parents were incredibly frugal and allowed each family member a modest number of shoes, much to the annoyance of my high school sister. Mr. Malcolm was the kind of customer who liked to converse while he browsed, and I was happy to oblige with a listening ear. Besides the vastness of his shoe collection, one of Mr. Malcolm's other frequent topics was the amount of racism still displayed in our country.

He'd say things like, "Do you get followed when you go to a store? I mean, a store other than your own? Because I do. My white buddy, Drew, and I will go shopping at a clothing store, and they let him wander all over the store with no concern, but follow me with their eyes, their feet, or both. I don't get it. What is *wrong* with people? The only thing I ever stole was a candy bar from a store when I was young, and my momma made me take it back and apologize to the store owner. Seriously! It makes a brother want to scream!" or, "Why do they sell ten kinds of light-skinned Band-Aids and only one kind of dark-skinned bandages? What? Like only one out of ten kids who get injured is a darker brother? And does that *one* darker bandage even *match* the skin color of the one who's buying it? It's just not right. Do things like this ever get you going?"

I just smiled and shook my head, as I hadn't experienced the same things that he had at that point in my life. Now, I feel like I am finally beginning to understand his frustrations. I realized that I missed seeing Mr. Malcolm. He came in faithfully to my family's store until the state put us all on lockdown, always treating me like a real person and looking me in the eye. What I wouldn't give to be back in our store, listening to one of Mr. Malcolm's tirades about the injustices in this world.

I sighed. Tensions were high and people were scared, my family included. We feared losing our business entirely, as we weren't sure when the lockdown would be over, and when it was over, we weren't sure if people would come back to our store. Luckily, my family valued frugality and saving money, so we had enough money saved to last us at least a year, but a year could go by pretty quickly. What would happen then?

Something I asked myself every day was this question: *What is something good I could be doing to help today?* Recently, that meant taking pictures of our inventory and putting them online, since that would be our only source of income for the time being. I had gotten more adept at marketing online with a few of the business marketing classes I had taken at a nearby college, for which my family was very grateful at this uncertain point in our lives.

When I finished with the last of our inventory, I again asked myself what I could be doing to help. Since we had been on lockdown, one of the things I did each morning was to read the newspaper from front to back, which I never used to have time to do. Prior to that, my reading was limited to a few general news stories and the majority of the business section. Now, reading the paper in its entirety, I noticed a section that I had never given much attention: the editorial section. For some reason, this section intrigued me. It wasn't just the variety of topics covered, but the passion with which people wrote. Many of the recent editorials were critiquing one party or another - usually the president, who typically gets blamed when something goes wrong in the country - for the inadequate response to the virus. Personally, I couldn't imagine being the head of our country during such a time as this. I couldn't imagine it and didn't envy him one bit. He would never be able to make everybody happy no matter what he did.

I sighed again. I was sick of the negativity that was going around. It wasn't just people losing their jobs or getting sick, but the lack of hope and amount of human skepticism that had been spreading faster than the virus itself. I had always been an optimistic person, an outlook that my family valued and exemplified to me. Something good I could do right now was to inspire people with words. More than ever, people had time to read right now. I took out my laptop and began to form the words of my first-ever editorial:

Rise up, America

My family owns a small shoe store in the bay business district. We have prided ourselves on providing quality shoes and exceptional service to our customers, and we will continue to do so as long as we are able.

We are also proud to be Chinese Americans. Recently, our heritage has been under attack, but moreover, America has been under attack, and not just by the virus. We have been attacking each other. Our fears have found their way to the surface of our lips with critical comments, name-calling, blaming, and hateful talk. My own father, a meek, mild, humble man, was recently sworn at on the bus for being a person of Chinese descent who was clearing his throat. I can't even begin to explain how much that hurt my heart to hear such verbal venom released by another human being.

I only mention this to help you to see what we are doing to each other. This is not the America our forefathers imagined when our country began. This is not the America my grandparents came to this country to encounter. This is not America. This is a lesser version of ourselves.

This is my challenge to you, fellow Americans: Rise. Rise up and ask yourself what good you can be doing each day. Rise up and help your fellow brother and sister, no matter the color of their skin. Share what you have with others. Look people in the eye. Speak words of hope to people. Love people well. What can you do to help your family today? Your neighbor? Your friends? The outcasts of society? Pick one thing each day and do it. It is by doing this one simple thing that will help us get through this pandemic together.

Recently, I saw a little girl around five or six years old picking up garbage around our neighborhood. Intrigued, I asked what she was doing and why. She replied that she was picking up garbage because it was something good that she could do that day. She confided to me that she had just watched *Frozen 2*, and her favorite part was when the troll said that when you didn't know what to do, you should just do the next right thing. Apparently, picking up garbage was her "next right thing."

I was inspired by this little girl. The spirit of this little girl resides in all of us. Can't we all just do the "next right thing" today? Rise up, America. We can get through this together.

- Chen Wu

Chapter 11

Penny

Dear Diary,

I am invisible. At least that's how I feel. And not the good kind of invisible. Not the superhero kind of invisibility that I can turn on and off in the blink of an eye to evade masked evildoers and save the world. The kind of invisible where people may detect me in their line of vision, but they don't really *see* me. They almost look through me. Past me. Around me. Anywhere but at me.

I didn't used to feel this way. In fact, in high school, I was one of those skinny and blonde, heavily-involved-in-school-activities kind of girls who other people thought had everything going for her. I had multiple groups of friends and more than a few boys who were interested in me, whom my father called my "entourage" during my teenage years. I earned straight-A's and made the High Honor Roll. I had an awesome family who supported me and made me laugh on a regular basis. I was told by multiple friends that they envied me because I seemed to have it all together.

At the time, I just shrugged my shoulders, not completely understanding what they meant. I've since discovered that it's always easier to see things from the outside looking in, but my age and life experiences hadn't taught me that yet. I did realize that I was lucky to have my faith, family, and friends ("the big three" as my family liked to say), and I *was* grateful for those things, but I didn't truly realize how fortunate I really was until later.

By the time I truly understood how many things were going my way, which was after I left the safety net of high school and was living in a dorm on my college campus, what I now term as "The Occurrence" happened. What I've since realized about seemingly having it all together is that there is more to fall apart. The more wood on the woodpile, the more pieces there are to tumble downward when you move the wrong one. The more apples in a bowl on the table, the more bruising and bumping as they fall onto the ground. That was me. Now I am bruised and broken, first on the outside and now on the inside, which is even worse because people can't really see it and therefore do not understand it. I've learned that no one can truly have it all together all of the time because we are human. Either we end up making a mistake or someone else makes the mistake that makes things unravel. In my case, the thread that pulled my entire tapestry of life apart was a seemingly innocent walk on my campus too late at night.

It was a gorgeous night. The moon was full and had a romantic sort of ring around it, calling me outside to share in its beauty. The air was still warm, given that it was that period of autumn that some people term "Indian summer" with its seemingly late blanket of warmth. I had been studying for hours and needed a break, and my window faced the moon that was speaking to me more directly than my books. The moonlight reminded me of a path around the small lake on our campus that was frequented by our students, and I decided that a walk around it was just the break that I needed.

As I laced up my tennis shoes and headed towards the lake, it didn't even occur to me to be on my guard. How naive I was, like many college freshman students who are riding the wings of freedom their first year being away from home. I walked slowly, admiring the reflection of the moon shimmering in the water. I imagined that I was a water bug who could ride the glistening moonlit path all the way to the moon itself, magically transporting me to the real object encased within the starry sky. Just as I imagined setting foot on the moon itself, after I had (in reality) reached the far end of the loop around the lake, I heard a rustle in the trees. I thought it was just a critter and didn't pay too much attention. Before I knew it, someone grabbed me from behind and dragged me into the woods.

What happened after that is kind of a blur. All I know is that I had been saving my virginity for Mr. Right and had it savagely stolen by Mr. Wrong.

Dear Diary,

Sorry for the abrupt stop in the last entry. I couldn't go on. It was too much to write about all at once, and just the thought of it made too many memories flood my brain. Not just word memories, but pictures, rolling like an inappropriately graphic movie through all synapse receptors within my head, flashing and blinding me with their ugliness. I simply had to stop and recuperate.

I prefer to call it "The Occurrence" instead of "The Rape" because rape is such a horrific word that seems to somewhat capture yet at the same time not completely encapsulate the essence of what happens to people. When I say "occurrence," it makes me feel like it was something that happened to me, but does not own me nor define me. It simply occurred. I refuse to let it dictate the rest of my life.

Whatever someone calls it doesn't really matter. What matters is that it happened and has changed me. In some ways, it has made life more difficult. I wrestle with many fears now that I never used to have, and it takes everything within me not to let my inner terrors overtake and dictate my life.

For one, I fear the woods now. I had a roommate in college who wouldn't go near the woods because she was extremely allergic to poison ivy. Allergic as in she would look at it and the stuff would seemingly jump from the ground onto her face. The rest of us on the dorm floor used to make fun of her for it and call her paranoid, but now I have a different perspective. Once you've been hurt, you want to avoid being hurt again at all costs. Once you've been traumatized, you avoid places of possible future trauma. What happened to me is like poison ivy. I never want to experience it again, which means I can't go anywhere near it. The woods are off limits to me now.

I also tremble at the thought of walking alone, especially in isolated places. A family member or friend accompanies me on outings if there is any chance of being left alone, which means I don't go as many places these days. I have gotten to the point where I can drive into the city with its very public places on my own, but anyplace where I could be left alone, especially after dark, is not an option for me any longer.

The dark. My worst fear. And it comes on the tail end of every day. Like clockwork, I can expect my greatest fear to come every twelve hours or so. Immediately following The Occurrence, night terrors took over my life. If I was lucky enough to fall asleep in the first place, which seemed to be a rare occurrence, I would wake up a few hours into my slumber, sweat-soaked and screaming, bolting up from my covers like HE was after me again. I had different versions of the same nightmare over and over again: I would be walking alone in the sunshine, and all of a sudden the sky would turn dark and a beast would come out of the woods, chasing me. I would run and run, exhausted and crying, but the beast would get closer and closer, its teeth bared, ready to devour me. That's when I would scream and wake up.

The problem was that I not only woke myself up, but my roommate and hall mates as well. My screaming, like a siren, awakened them all, and there was nothing I could do to prevent it. My roommate, Bekkah, would get out of her bed and run over to mine, shaking me and calling me back to reality. She'd keep repeating, "Penny, you're safe," eventually drawing me back to the real world with her soothing tone. Bekkah, who was one of the few people I told about what happened to me, had become a close friend to me in the first few months of school, and I appreciated her kindness following The Occurrence. The rest of my hall mates, who weren't informed of the trauma I had undergone, didn't extend me the same sympathy and kindness. I heard them whisper things like, "What is wrong with her? She screams like every night!" Their annoyed stares and cutting comments made it difficult to want to stay at school. That, combined with the fact that I wasn't able to concentrate on my classes any longer, eventually forced me to go home. I had never quit anything in my life, and now I hadn't finished my first semester of college.

December 20

Dear Diary,

It's almost Christmas, but I can't quite get into the celebratory mood. Christmas has always been my favorite holiday, but somehow it's different this year. It's hard to explain it in words, but all of the holiday cheer remains outside of me. On the periphery. Just out of my grasp. Elusive. I try to let it permeate my exterior and move into the inner realms of my spirit, but there seems to be some sort of force field blocking any rays of sunshine from getting to my heart. I play Christmas music, but it only makes me sad because the joy that bubbles out of the singer's mouth somehow stays within the music; it never transfers over to me, no matter how much I try to feel it.

I've been home for about a month now. It feels strange to be home. It's like I don't fit anywhere right now. I should be at college right now, but the thought of being there terrifies me right now. I also should feel "right at home" while being in the home I've lived in since childhood, but things have changed since The Occurrence. *I've* changed since it happened. My own bedroom seems foreign to me, as if someone else has lived there over the past eighteen years. My high school friends have come home from college for Christmas break, but when I hang out with them, it's as if I don't know them any longer and they don't truly know me.

It almost seems as if I am pretending amidst someone else's friends. I'm like Goldilocks trying out all of the chairs and none are the right size. None of the porridge is the right temperature. None of the beds are comfortable enough. Nothing in life seems to fit any longer.

My family notices the difference in me. They pretend like they haven't noticed, but they can't fool me. I can see it in their facial expressions when they attempt to draw me out of my trauma-imposed turtle shell with their many questions, waiting for answers that are usually one word and long in coming. As they wait expectantly, their forced smiles eventually droop with the ticking of the clock. I can feel it in the silence that ensues when I enter a room. Whatever conversation that was occurring is hushed. I know that means they have been talking about me, but I realize it's because they are trying to figure out what to do with me. How can they possibly figure *that* out when I don't even know what to do with me?

I think the tipping point for my family was when we all went to get the family Christmas tree. My parents took the front two seats while my two older brothers and I piled in the back, just like when we were growing up. I put on my best smile and bantered with my brothers, trying to get into the holiday spirit. We arrived at the tree farm, looking for the "perfect tree," which ended up being a large Douglas fir, as usual. We (meaning my dad and my two brothers) chopped it down with our trusty axe, which the men always insist on using instead of the much faster chainsaw, and we tied the tree on top of the car to head for home.

For the time being, it seemed like everything might just be back to normal again, but then we started decorating the tree. My mom cued up the music, and just as Burl Ives got to how "holly jolly" of a Christmas it was, I pricked my finger on an ornament hook and blood started coming out of my finger. Blood. Just seeing it reminded me of The Occurrence. I was instantly transported back to the woods with my attacker, and the ounce of control I had been able to exercise in my life dissolved instantly. I started screaming and crying, and my family wasn't able to console me.

They ended up bringing me to the hospital, where, after being given a relaxant, I was assigned to a psychiatrist. After talking with my family about The Occurrence and what happened to me while putting up the Christmas tree, my diagnosis was post-traumatic stress disorder, or PTSD. I wasn't aware that PTSD wasn't just a war veteran diagnosis. My doctor had to explain that *any* traumatic event (or series of events, in some cases), whether war-related or not, could cause this disorder. She went on to say that, besides soldiers, one of the other big categories of patients were ones who had experienced some sort of sexual trauma. Those who had experienced some sort of medical trauma, such as an accident or repeated medical emergencies, also commonly were diagnosed with PTSD. Who knew so many different types of people could be traumatized by so many different things?

Anyway, it made me feel considerably better to be given a diagnosis, an *explanation*, as to why I had been feeling the way I had the past few months. It explained the nightmares that left me screaming, the panic attacks, and the intense anxiety I felt on a regular basis. It made me feel at least somewhat normal again to know I wasn't alone in what I was feeling. I have been put on some medicines that are supposed to help with my anxiety, overall mood, and nightmares at night. Here's to hoping for good things...

January 27

Dear Diary,

Let's play "Good News, Bad News." Good News: My medicine is working. My night terrors have decreased and I am sleeping better, which has helped my days go better, as well. It's a wonder what a good night's sleep will do for a person. I had almost forgotten what it felt like to be well-rested. I guess my mom, who has always gotten after me to get more sleep, was right all these years. Perhaps my youth leader's mantra of "You can sleep when you're dead!" is not the best philosophy, after all is said and done.

Besides getting better sleep, my overall mood has evened out. I don't feel the intense lows any longer. Immediately following The Occurrence, I felt like I was in the "depths of despair," as Anne of Green Gables, one of my favorite fictional characters, labeled it, and I couldn't get out. A heavy blanket was covering me, and I couldn't find my way out from underneath it. Moreover, I found myself *wanting* to stay under the blanket, hiding from the world and other people's stares and questions, which was even worse.

My overall anxiety level has decreased. Things still frighten me, but I am able to rationalize why I *shouldn't* be afraid, which is most of the battle. My brain is once again able to decide for itself what is worrisome and what is not. I like that small sense of control that I have regained. I can't let fear win, and my medicine gives me the weapon of my rational mind back so I can fight against the anxious thoughts that used to dominate my thinking.

Now for the bad news. Since the old blanket of sadness and anxiety has lifted, a new one has taken its place: the cloak of numbness. Not feeling things too deeply means not feeling anything deeply enough. Therapeutic indifference. Curative impassiveness. Medicinal apathy. Now, when I feel happy, it is as if the sunshine is muted. I am able to see the sunshine but not feel the warmth of it. I am able to climb the mountain, but the mountain-top euphoria is left to the other climbers.

Then there is the weight gain. My doctors warned me of it, but I somehow didn't believe them. In my mind, that was something that happened to *other* people, not to me. I've never been able to gain weight in my life. I've always been active, which, aiding my swift metabolism, forgave any of the late-night snacks I used to inhale in typical teenage fashion. Now, whatever I eat seems to *stick* to my body. It has only been about ten pounds so far, but ten pounds in a little over a month makes me nervous for what is to come.

March 17

Dear Diary,

It is Saint Patrick's Day. A day of luck. A day where everyone is "Irish" and people celebrate their kinship in a sea of green. I am wearing a green t-shirt, one that says "Feeling Lucky 5k" on it from a road race I ran a few years ago with a couple of high school friends. I have mixed feelings about the words on my shirt.

I *am* lucky to have survived The Occurrence. I know in my heart of hearts that He Who Must Not Be Named (I borrowed this from *Harry Potter*, which I've been reading lately) could have killed me in the woods that night. I could have been wiped off the face of the earth in that single moment. My family and friends would have been devastated. I would never have had a chance to pursue any of my dreams. But I was left to LIVE, and I try to remind myself of that each and every day.

Therein lies the problem. I have to intentionally *remind* myself each day that I am fortunate to have survived. It's a choice every day. I don't actually *feel* lucky. I know that life is about choices and I choose gratitude over despair, but I wish I could just feel it on my own. In reality, fear is what I feel on a daily basis. I feel fearful that I will be hurt again. I feel anxious about what the next day will bring, though I have Philippians 4:6-7–"Do not be anxious about anything, but in every situation, by prayer and petition, with thanksgiving, present your requests to God. And the peace of God, which transcends all understanding, will guard your hearts and your minds in Christ Jesus"–taped to my bathroom mirror and repeat it daily like it's some sort of mantra. I am still waiting to truly feel that "peace that transcends all understanding." My therapist, Marie, who I've been seeing since the blood-induced screaming incident at Christmas, tells me that I will eventually feel peaceful, but it will take time.

I also feel overweight and frumpy. My medicine is causing weight gain at a rapid pace. I gained ten points in January and 15 pounds in February. It is beginning to change the shape of my body and even my face. Everything is just a little bit rounder and softer now. I know I should be exercising more, but then I either have to be outside by myself or inside a building with other people, neither of which sounds appealing to me at the present moment. How ironic that many anti-anxiety medications, which do help even out people's moods, also make people gain weight, causing even more anxiety about the way people look and feel. It's like an endless cycle. I can either not take my medicine and feel like crud mentally or take my medicine and feel like crud physically. Sigh.

Happy St. Patrick's Day. Here's to truly *feeling* lucky again...someday.

June 1

Dear Diary,

June is here, and with it comes the promise of summer in all of its sunshiny glory. I am hoping that the sunshine permeates my body and thaws the layer of medicinal indifference that has made its wall around my innermost thoughts. I want to experience the elation of happiness, not the watered-down version of it that I have felt over the course of the past five months.

My friends have begun their pilgrimages home from college, and with them comes the air of expectation. Friendship is an amazing gift, but with it comes certain...obligations. Friends *expect* to get together often and have it feel like old times. They *expect* all of us to share our recent life mishaps and successes, the first of which I have in spades but don't feel comfortable sharing with the group and the latter of which I don't have enough, as of late, to share. They *expect*...the girl I was when we all left for college. Not the Penny who was used, ransacked, and discarded like garbage.

I have seen the surprise on their faces at my appearance. It's in the first few seconds—between the moment their eyes take me in and when their brain registers what they are seeing, reminding them not to stare–that I feel the most ashamed about my body. Every month since January, when I began taking my anti-anxiety medications, I have gained at least ten pounds. In total, 60 pounds have had to find a place to reside on my 5'7" frame. The weight has visibly changed the contour and feel of my body. I have had to purchase new clothes, which, fortunately for me, my mother–the shopping queen–was more than willing to assist me in doing.

My weight gain, though uninvited and unwanted, has made me more keenly aware of an entire segment of the population that is often overlooked: the overweight. Now that I have become one of that group, I feel not only the physical weight of the pounds, but the social gravity that comes with it. What I've found is that most people typically aren't outright rude or hurtful to overweight people, but rather, the damage comes in the form of overlooking. Not seeing. Ignoring. Making people feel invisible. When at a store, the skinny and beautiful ones seem to get noticed and helped first. When walking down the street, men's eyes skip over me and rest on the others whose exteriors are more appealing than mine. When things like bathroom stalls, amusement park rides, and airplanes are constructed, they obviously don't have the needs of the overweight in mind. In fact, on a recent trip to an indoor amusement park, I saw a mother attempt to sit by her child on a roller coaster, and she discovered, to her horror, that she wasn't able to actually *fit* in the seat. Mortified, she exited the ride, not able to hide her shame and embarrassment. My heart went out to her. I resolved then and there to begin to truly *see* and *value* those who are largely ignored by the majority: the overweight, the aged, the mentally handicapped, the mentally ill, the ethnically diverse, and the social outcasts. After what I've gone through, I've realized that people just want to be noticed. Truly seen. Listened to. Valued. I could do that. One by one, we can *all* do that, can't we?

Sometimes, when I am being introspective, which happens a lot lately, I think about my name. Pennies, when new, are shiny and beautiful. Children are elated to get one, content with any form of currency. Even adults will notice the sheen of a recently-minted penny. Then, as time goes on, pennies change hands and lose their luster. The oxygen in the air changes their physical composition, oxidizing the outside of the penny until it looks dingy and dull. Dirty. Ignored. Left on the ground and trampled. If I'm being honest, that's how I've often felt following The Occurrence.

But here's the thing I know about pennies: They can be cleaned. I remember a science experience that we did once in elementary school. We were all assigned to bring in the dirtiest pennies that we could find. My teacher, Mr. Ross, told us that the dirtier the pennies were, the better the outcome of the experiment. We were to look on the ground, in our piggy banks, and in our parents' change containers. I found a few that were so dingy that it was difficult to even see the outline of President Lincoln. *Perfect*, I had thought. *Just like Mr. Ross asked us to find.*

We all brought our sullied pennies in for the experiment, excited to see what would happen to them. Mr. Ross went first, demonstrating the experiment with one of the crustiest-looking pennies I had ever seen. In my head, I was thinking, *There's no way that penny will come clean. It's too dirty!* Then, magically, before our very eyes, the vinegar and salt solution did its trick. I couldn't wait to try the experiment myself, and to my amazement, my dingy pennies came out clean. Just like that. They just needed the right ingredients and a little time.

It's odd how often I have thought back to that experiment since The Occurrence. At the time, a penny-cleaning session wasn't exactly an earth-shattering incident to an elementary student, and if I'm being honest, I hadn't given one iota of thought about the experiment until recently. Now, I can't seem to shake the mental image of the dirty penny going into the solution and the shiny penny coming out of it. I am that penny. I am that Penny. I may feel used and dirty now, but I have the hope that I will someday be shiny and clean again. It will just take the right ingredients for my Penny-cleaning solution and some time.

August 27

Dear Diary,

One of the "ingredients" that has been life-changing for me this summer has been my friend, Jody. She is like the energizer bunny who bangs on her drum of encouragement day after day. The ironic thing is that we weren't that close in high school. She was in my graduating class and in my youth group, but we always ran in different friend circles. In fact, when I was simultaneously looking forward to and dreading my high school friends coming back from college, Jody wasn't even on my radar.

About a week into June, I received a message on my phone and opened it. I saw Jody's name and profile picture pop up. Curious, I clicked on her message:

Hey, Penny!
I know we don't know each other super well, but I recently came back from college and am looking for an exercise partner. I was racking my brain to think of someone who might be interested, and your name popped into my head. I don't know what your schedule is or what your exercise preferences are, but I am flexible and like almost anything. Just throwing it out there. Let me know!
- Jody

I remember being somewhat confused, wondering if she had meant to message someone else instead of me, but there was the message with my name on top of it. After the initial puzzlement wore off, the thought of an exercise partner got me kind of excited. Hadn't I been nervous to exercise outside by myself? Hadn't I been lamenting the fact that I was gaining weight and wanted to change something in my life? The answer to both questions was a resounding YES.

I messaged her back right away:

Hey, Jody!

Long story short, I have been wanting to exercise lately but haven't wanted to go alone. I would actually love to exercise with you! I am up for almost anything, but a few of my favorites are rollerblading and biking. I used to run quite a bit, but I haven't gone for quite a while and am out of shape. Honestly, it's like you read my mind or something because I have really been wanting to make a few positive changes in my life lately, and this is one of them. Let's schedule a time and place!

- Penny

Since then, we have been meeting multiple times a week. Sometimes we bike, sometimes we rollerblade, and other times we just walk and talk. I don't know how else to say it, but meeting with her has changed me. For one, having someone to keep me accountable gets me out of bed in the morning. Following The Occurrence, I slept for long periods of time as one of my coping mechanisms to deal with my pain (as my therapist stated it), but now I have a reason to get up in the mornings. Knowing I would be disappointing her if I didn't show up is reason enough to leave the warmth and security of my covers each morning.

Besides the accountability factor, my body has become more fit. It's been a slow process, and I still don't look like I did before The Occurrence, but some of the pounds have come off and my body actually *feels* healthy once again. At least now I can look in the mirror and be happy with the progress I have made, even if I still have a ways to go.

The biggest difference has been emotionally. Following The Occurrence, I was an emotional wreck. I couldn't sleep for fear of being attacked again in my nightmares, and the lack of sleep negatively affected my emotional capacity while I was awake. I still have nightmares, but they are less frequent. Pleasant dreams have even found their way back into my sleep cycle, aiding me in my quest for that elusive full night's sleep that has only recently become a possibility. The simple act of talking with another person releases my emotional baggage. It's difficult to explain, but an enormous rain cloud of shame with lightning bolts of self-judgment seems to linger over those who have been sexually violated, and having a friend who truly listens has been the gentle breeze that chases those clouds away. The sun has come out again, and the endorphins released during exercising have helped to even out my mood for the rest of the day, flooding my brain with the possibility of feeling hopeful once again.

Hope. Possibility. Those two words coexisting prove that miracles can happen. The real Penny seems to be crawling out of her hiding place, blinking brightly in the face of the sunshine, slowly standing and dusting herself off as a smile at the wonder of being alive slowly stretches across her face.

After: Take the Challenge

Tag! You're it! Your turn. This isn't a sit-around-after-reading-and-do-nothing kind of book. This is a wake-up call, and for some of you, it might be your last wake-up call before it's too late.

This book has been filled with the stories of people who had something important to say and finally found the courage to say it. As an author, I can only hope and pray that this has given you a different perspective. Everyone has a story. We can't avoid that life is complicated and messy. That's because we are human. We all make mistakes, and many of those mistakes have disastrous and far-reaching consequences. Whether you have been the offender or offended, there is always the hope for redemption. We have the chance to make things right...but only if we take it.

Whom have you been avoiding? Who has incurred your wrath and needs your forgiveness instead of your bitterness? Who has changed your life and you haven't said anything? Who has been the source of your judgment and could use a little grace instead? Who needs to hear the life-changing phrase "I love you" from your very lips?

Dismiss any excuses that are flooding your brain right now. The human brain is the great manipulator and self-excuser. So long as you're breathing, it's never too late. So long as the other person with whom you wish to speak is still alive, you have a chance to make things right with them. If that isn't possible, so long as the human heart has the ability to forgive, you have the opportunity to release pain and bitterness by forgiving yourself or someone else.

Carpe diem! Seize the day! As the saying goes, "If you woke up this morning, then you've been given another chance." This day is a gift you don't have the luxury to waste because you aren't guaranteed the gift of tomorrow. Tell someone how you really feel. If you can't say it aloud, then write your thoughts down on paper. I am personally far more eloquent on paper than I am orally. The point is that you make the effort to say the important things to the people who are truly important to you in order to make your life and the lives of those around you more meaningful.

What if the other person doesn't respond in the way I wish? you may wonder. That might happen. If I am being completely honest, that *will* happen to some of you. The other person might not forgive you. There might be some hard conversations that ensue. There might be tears. The other person may ignore you and not respond at all. But...at least you will have done your part and will no longer have regrets. As I always tell my students and my children, you can only control YOU. The other person might need their own space and time to come around (and maybe a lot of prayer). Do your part. Make the effort. Pay it forward.

Before it's too late.

The Author: Challenge Accepted

How hypocritical would it be to write such a book and not write to my own family? That would be like buying chocolate and just looking at it or purchasing a vacation and not boarding the plane.

I have a confession: I wrote this chapter first but decided it would go last. The other chapters contain fictional characters created in the depths of my imagination and experience, but this chapter is as real as it gets.

*   *   *   *   *   *   *   *   *   *   *   *

It's funny how your personality starts busting out somewhere between infancy and toddlerhood, and much of it stays the same into adulthood. I have seen this with other people's children and with myself. How much of your personality is genetically programmed into your DNA and how much of it is nurtured? Can the human body and brain ever be fully understood?

As a child, I grew up on a ten-acre hobby farm with a carpenter father, stay-at-home mother (who sold hand-made crafts and Park Lane Jewelry on the side), and three other siblings. My two older brothers took the protector-in-public-but-tormentor-at-home role very seriously, while my younger sister calmly and sweetly avoided engaging in their mischief that more often than not was rerouted to me. It was partially my fault, I admit. I was, to put it bluntly, a spazz. I could be reduced to tears in a matter of minutes, whether it was because one of my brothers had convinced me that I was hatched from an egg and then adopted or because they were torturing one of my dolls that I couldn't seem to rescue. I vividly recall one of my dolls with a noose around her neck, swaying gently from a barn rafter, just above my reach. It took me a long time to learn that ignoring them did the trick. Once they lost their easy prey, they looked to other pastures for their fun. They have since told me that they were just preparing me for real life, just "making me tougher," which was probably not their intention but happened in the process anyway.

I have always been infatuated by stories. My dad has always been a storyteller, and the ideas he came up with could have been the subject of storybooks if he had taken the time to write them all down. He would often formulate a story over the course of a couple of weeks and then give us children a countdown until "spooky story night" or some other such title. We would anxiously count the days away until story night finally arrived—much to the chagrin of my mother, who often was awakened during the night by one of us having a nightmare stemming from one of Dad's stories—and pile like little piggies into one of the beds, giggling and squealing in anticipation. Since then, my father has published multiple books of short stories, and his love of story has been passed down to me, as I have become an English teacher and an author.

Now, with a husband and two children of my own, I see the power of story in a new light. My daughter, Paisley, absolutely thrives on stories. On many car rides, she begs, "Tell us a story!" and I am more than happy to oblige. She usually supplies the basic framework ("tell a story about an animal mix-up with a cheetah") and away I go. If she has a friend in the car, she still asks for a story and conspiratorially leans over to her friend to whisper, "My mom tells the *best* stories." She devours books every night before bed, and as we read together, I sense the way stories stitch people together with the thread of a shared experience.

Each of us writes a story with our lives, too, without ever putting pen to paper. I hope my life story is one my children will remember fondly. I hope the words I say on a daily basis uplift the spirit, offer hope, and teach perseverance that my children will one day need to survive and thrive in this ever-changing world. As do all parents, I hope that I will be around to personally witness their transformation from sweet babes to adults, but, unfortunately, none of us are guaranteed that time. I know if my parents had died when I was young, I would have clung to any words they had said aloud, and, after the memories started to fade with time, I would have treasured any written words that were left for me. I would have cherished any cards or letters, putting them in a special place to be read over and over again. Words are a gift that survives long past death, and I want to leave those I love most with that most precious gift. And so I write to my humorous husband, Josh; my spirited nine-year-old daughter, Paisley; and my tender-hearted five-year-old, August:

Dear Josh,

I know you dislike sitting still and have an aversion to lengthy reading, so I will keep this short and sweet. Besides explaining all of the logistical stuff for sustaining a household and raising two children (that will be a different letter, as that one is much more boring with financial and organizational advisement), there are really two things I would want to say to you:

First, thank you for always loving me...no matter what. If you will recall (though you won't want me to remind you of this), there was a time before we were married where I was deciding between you and someone else. One of the big things that swayed me in your direction was that I knew you would love me deeply and without reserve forever and always. You have always loved me for me—despite my intensely independent nature and overzealous drive to accomplish way more than humanly possible each and every day—and I knew I could always count on that love. You have never given me cause to wonder if you were being unfaithful, and that is a gift in itself...the gift of never-ceasing, far-reaching, ever-faithful, utterly-devoted love. For that I thank you. I have always felt it and have always felt grateful for it. As I tell you every day, I love you, too...lots and lots and tons and tons.

Second, I want you to know that I admire you. I may have never said this aloud to you, but I do nonetheless. I admire you for so many things. For one, you are smart...way smarter than you let on. You are always able to figure things out, whether it be a project we are working on for the house or a people issue. You are able to see the situation for what it is and think of outside-the-box, tangible solutions for almost any problem. You have this uncanny ability to read people and situations for what they are, which I have discovered is a rare quality to possess. Besides that, you are helpful. People call you all of the time to help them with things because you are strong, willing, and able. I know that I have joked that you are so busy helping everyone else that you don't have time to help me at home, but deep down I admire that you strive to love people by helping them when they need it most. It's a good way to be. Lastly, I admire you because you are one tough cookie. You have persevered through so much with your leg surgeries and rheumatoid arthritis, and I know you will continue to persevere through whatever else life may throw at you because you are a survivor. Remember that God has always been your anchor, so continue to depend on Him. You also have an amazing family and group of friends who really love and support you. Don't forget that. Even tough cookies need help and support.

Remember that real love never dies. Though my body will die someday, love always lives on. As Mitch Albom says in his book *The Five People You Meet in Heaven*, "Lost love is still love." Remember that. Keep on keepin' on, and always feel the love that I have had and continue to have for you.

Love Always (Tons and Tons),

Rach

My Spirited Paisley,

When I think of you, I think of many things. I think of rainbows of color and beautiful butterflies. I think of your love for stories and how we snuggle every night while reading books. I think of a Mustang horse running wild and free, spirit untamed and without fear.

As I tell you often, you are my miracle. You convinced me to face my fears of being pregnant and giving birth (which, trust me, at the time seemed very real and immensely scary). After you were born, I would just stare at you and think what a miracle you were (and still are), from your tiny nose to your sweet, sweet toes. If you slept long at night, I would run in and make sure my miracle was still breathing. I thank God every day for my miracle, as you bring so much light and life into this world.

It makes me smile that we share a love for running. I didn't truly discover my love of running until late in high school, but you seem to have discovered your passion early. One of your very first full sentences was when you were two and you said, "You find me race. You watch; you clap." So I found you a few kids' races, and now you have already run a 5K (three miles)! I couldn't even run one mile when I was your age! Amazing! Keep running, my wild and free Mustang girl. Run and feel the wind in your hair and the sun on your face and never let anyone tell you to stop. Run towards your dreams and away from bad decisions. Run towards your faith and take others with you. Run, girl. Just run.

Remember a few things. Remember that I always love you, and that can never be taken away, even by death. Love lives on. When you go for a run, remember my love. When you snuggle in your covers at night, remember my love. When you ride your horse in our arena with your hair flying in the wind, remember my love. When you play outside on the farm with your brother and all of our farm critters, remember my love.

Also, remember your faith. God will always love you and will never leave you. Cling to Jesus and you will always have the best friend anyone could ever have. He is always there for you, day or night. He knows what you have been through and what you are going through. He loves you no matter what.

Keep shining your light, my brave girl. Shine it brightly for all to see.

I love you, Sweet P!

Mommy

My Sweet Auggie,

When I think of you, I think of sweet hugs and floppy-wristed waves. I think of gut-busting giggles when you get tickled and the pitter-patter of feet as you run by. I think of your love for animals, especially your "stuffies" (stuffed animals), and the way you can make every animal sound. I think of the sweet way you sing songs like "Twinkle, Twinkle Little Star."

You were born a strong boy. On your birthday in the hospital, in the wee morning hours on August 5th, you raised your head off of my shoulder and held it up for a moment before laying it back down. I remember being astounded at your strength, even on day one of your existence.

You were born at just over nine pounds and have always been what I would call "solid." Whenever people pick you up, they comment something to the effect of,

"Wow. He's heavier than he looks. He's a solid little guy." Even at a young age, you are a solid pillar of strength. Use that strength for good things, Auggie. Use it to help your family. Use it to help your neighbors. Use it to help people you come across who need assistance in more ways than one.

Moreover, let your strength be both outer and inner. Have the inner strength to do the right thing, even when no one else is looking and you could easily get away with doing the wrong thing. Have the fortitude to persevere through difficult times. Be a man of integrity whose goodness shines to others, inspiring faith and hope in both God and mankind. As I pray for you often, "Be strong and courageous! Do not be afraid or discouraged, for the Lord your God is with you wherever you go" (Joshua 1:9). Use your strength for good things, my solid boy.

Always remember that you are so loved...by your family and by God. Live in the knowledge of that love and let it overflow from your life into the lives of others around you. You bring joy to this world with your sweet smiles, warm hugs, and contagious laughter, and I am proud to be your mother.

Love Always,

Mommy

SHARE YOUR OWN JUST-IN-CASE-I-DIE STORIES!

If you have verbally told or written to any loved ones about the things you want them to know just in case YOU die, I would love to hear your stories!

Please email me at rachelsnorby@gmail.com to share your own just-in-case-I-die stories. With your permission, your story could even be featured on my author website at rachelnorby.com!

Let's start a movement!

#justincaseidie

Book Club Questions

"Before"

-Why do you think people sometimes don't say the things they really feel to the people they care about most? What kinds of things do YOU tend to not say even though you feel them strongly?

-Words are powerful. Describe a time when you have witnessed either the positive OR the negative power of words.

"Nick"

-Nick comments, "What a deceiver you are, Alcohol. What a normalized, unobtrusive liar cloaked in sleek-looking bottles and mesmerizingly shiny cans," since his drinking ended up being a negative experience in his life. Have your experiences with alcohol been positive, negative, or both? Explain.

-Has alcohol ever become a problem for you or anyone you know? Besides the obvious addictiveness aspects of alcohol, why do you think people have trouble STOPPING drinking, even when it has become a problem in their lives?

"Jade"

-Out of the many mistakes human beings make, infidelity is universally considered one of the "worst" and is incredibly difficult to forgive. Did you find yourself having sympathy for Jade or not?

-Do you think everyone is susceptible to cheating? Explain your answer.

"Coach Nova"

-Have you or anyone else that you know ever been in a serious car accident? If so, were there any lasting effects?

-As a reader, you can tell that Coach Novus is respected by many. In your opinion, what makes a person respected and/or WORTHY of respect? Who do YOU respect and why?

"Rue"

-Abortion is a highly sensitive and often inflammatory topic. What were you thinking as you read Rue's statement, "In hindsight, after years of mulling it over in my brain, I have concluded that the real debate about abortion is actually over whether or not it's *permissible*, which is completely different than the typical discussion of whether it's morally right or wrong"?

-Rue's abortion has greatly affected her life, but she has learned to forgive herself. Why is it often more difficult to forgive oneself than it is to forgive other people?

"Max[well]"

-Names have power. What significance does your name have? Have you had any nicknames that you've either liked or disliked?

-Max seems to simultaneously want his dad to come home and feels angry that his dad abandoned him. Why do you think people often desire the approval/love of a parent who is not physically (or emotionally) present?

"Ruby"

-Most people WANT to grow old together when they get married. Besides death or illness, why do you think so many people don't end up staying married for life?

-Have you personally known anyone affected by Alzheimer's Disease? If so, how did it affect that person's life and the lives of their loved ones? If you had to choose, would YOU rather lose function of your mind or body when you get older and why?

"Robert"

-Have you ever had a photograph (or a different medium/ work of art) "wreck" you, as Flora claims her brother's photography does? If so, explain.

-Robert's photography/artistry connects him to his lost loved ones and other people. What power(s) do you feel art has? Give an example from your life or someone you know.

"Lily"

-Has your life been affected in any way by divorce? If so, how?

-Lily finds her "outlet" by creating art. The book says, **"Art turns wounds into light."** Is art an outlet for you? If not, what IS an outlet for you when you are upset?

"Millie"

-Is there anything that you will drive a sizable distance to purchase because it is so good OR because you like the environment of that place? If so, what is it and WHY will you drive for it?

-Millie is not only known for her raspberries, but for her "berry wise" bits of wisdom. Who would you consider to be a "wise" person in your life and why? Do you think other people would say YOU are wise?

"Chen"

-The COVID-19 pandemic has affected our world in many ways. What have been some positives and negatives that have come out of facing the virus and/or other recent hardships?

-Chen and his family have been the target of some negative racial remarks. What were your thoughts when you read this chapter? What is at least ONE thing that you feel people can and should do in order to help tackle racial division and promote reconciliation?

"Penny"

-Sexual assault affects many people. What do you think we can personally do to help lessen the number of assaults and/or help the victims recover?

-Penny says that her assault and subsequent weight gain have made her aware of segments of the population that have largely been ignored. Who do you feel are the MOST ignored segments of our population and why? What can YOU personally do to start "seeing" these forgotten people?

"After"

-It is said that books have the power to change lives. Have you ever read a book that transformed you as a person?

-What do you feel compelled to do after reading this book and why? GO DO IT!

About the Author

 Avid reader, writer, and runner, Rachel Norby has authored multiple inspirational books that reinforce the power of hope in a world plagued by hardship. Currently residing in Mora, Minnesota with her husband and two children, Rachel balances writing and speaking engagements with her youth work as a high school English teacher, youth director at her church, and cross country running coach. Visit rachelnorby.com for more information.

Other books by Rachel Norby:

- *Let the Rain Fall* (2010): a work of fiction

- *The Good One* (2013): a work of fiction

- *The Long Way Around* (2016): narrative nonfiction (based on a true story)